VALENTINO'S CURSE
THE SHEIK RETURNS

LARRY L. DRELLER

Outskirts Press, Inc.
Denver, Colorado

This is a work of fiction. The events and characters described herein are imaginary and are not intended to refer to specific places or living persons. The opinions expressed in this manuscript are solely the opinions of the author and do not represent the opinions or thoughts of the publisher. The author has represented and warranted full ownership and/or legal right to publish all the materials in this book.

Valentino's Curse
The Sheik Returns
All Rights Reserved.
Copyright © 2011 Larry L. Dreller
v2.0

Cover Illustration © 2011 Outskirts Press, Inc. All Rights Reserved. Used with permission.

This book may not be reproduced, transmitted, or stored in whole or in part by any means, including graphic, electronic, or mechanical without the express written consent of the publisher except in the case of brief quotations embodied in critical articles and reviews.

Outskirts Press, Inc.
http://www.outskirtspress.com

ISBN: 978-1-4327-6425-8

Outskirts Press and the "OP" logo are trademarks belonging to Outskirts Press, Inc.

PRINTED IN THE UNITED STATES OF AMERICA

The Curse Begins

CHICAGO, 1926

Reba Walizuski rolled her mass onto a protesting dinette chair while sighing dramatically to a non-existent audience. It had been another long night with too much on her mind--important decisions and another unwanted commitment.

A sudden gush of searing stomach acid mixed with an early morning headache churned an already bilious and nervous stomach, a regular occurrence in a horrific year. Despite the growing distance from time and events of the previous year, she continued to be numbed from the poisons of anxiety and depression which had escalated into a very trying year, to put it mildly.

Her beloved husband Peter, had been dead for almost two years now, killed while switching track in the central Chicago train yards, a horrible nightmare--barely enough remains secured for a funeral, and the bills, mountains of past due bills; her depression accelerated with acute frustration over things she could not control, especially hating the loss of any control.

Fears of destitution and ending up on the mean streets of an uncaring Chicago, alone and begging; chills began racking her for the thousandth time since Peter had passed. She pulled a yellowed, lace bordered handkerchief from the tight arm cuff of her faded flowered housecoat and dabbed daintily at the corners of her eyes, careful not to smear her mascara. Reba was startled that she could still cry, sure that any tears she had left dried-up the day Peter had died leaving her poor in a cold, indifferent world.

Reba knew she would have to eventually accept the offer of marriage from Peter's best friend, John Tonapolski, whether she wanted to or not. She had stalled him long enough while weighing the benefits of a proposed marriage, afraid that her indecision would drive him away. John was an impatient hot-head, five years younger than she, topped with abundant clown-like blazing red hair and riveting green eyes, masking a sometimes nasty male immaturity and rotten disposition. Recently in bed, after another particularly hot lovemaking tussle, John had grunted out his final demand—Reba would give him the answer of marriage next week, with no more stalling, or he would move on. He hadn't hidden what he expected from a marriage: sex, clean clothes, cooking, children, and even respectability. Perhaps love could even enter the picture in time.

Reba did realize that her very survival and comfort was at stake—and she was growing desperate to have these financial weights lifted from her sagging shoulders as soon as possible. In the positive assets of her acceptance to his approval, he could be generous and open-handed, and was most certainly a passionate, aggressive lover in bed. She certainly could smooth away his rough edges in a short period of time—all men were set ups under the easy hand of an experienced woman. Reba could do much worse than to marry this younger man, knowing it would work out, it had to.

She carried dreams of a north shore cottage far away from the city, where she would be able to gain self-respect and status by joining a woman's league and perhaps a garden club. She would even have his children, two or three--she was young enough, raising them to be upper crust swells, status which John and she could never really hope to attain--at least in this lifetime. Why not a new start? A new life? The meager widow's railroad pension was not enough to survive on, and the bills, well, she knew she would have to give in to John's offer, more sooner than later. Worse things could happen to a lonely and impoverished widow than another marriage, and taking an exit from being destitute in a dirty uncaring Chicago.

John could certainly be considered a prime "Grade A" catch: younger than she, boyishly handsome--tall, solidly built, with tendencies of being a go-getter and wheeler dealer. He came with a railroad supervisor's job and had more money salted away than Peter could ever have dreamed of in his honest God ordained life, and strangely, John had never been married or engaged before they met, hence, she would be able to break him in properly like she had Peter. Yes, he was indeed quite a catch, his main drawback being a vicious temper competing with his flaming red hair.

Reba's employment at Rossi's Tea Room on Prairie Avenue had helped to wipe out a minute portion of Peter's gambling and disastrous stock investment debts, but trying to keep ahead of the loan sharks had been next to impossible; she involuntarily shuddered with thoughts of the last threat she had received from these blood suckers, remembering that an already long overdue payment was due the following week at double the interest. God, she wished she was better at sending spells and curses! She'd make their balls fall off. She knew she had the "gift", but was still honing her skills on how to activate these powers. She wished she had paid more attention to the lessons from her mother. She had first worked as a dishwasher in the tea room after Peter's death and in less than four months had been able to make a passable wage as an apprentice reader, with decent tips now, from reading tea leaves and Tarot cards. Madame Rossi said that she had a special knack in pleasing the demanding rich biddies that came in for vacuous psychic readings of potential sordid affairs and stock market tips. Reba knew she had much more to offer, in time, but for now she would have to be patient, knowing that it would come—then…?

Lately, it had been difficult keeping up with requests to "see" what Rudy Valentino was doing in the otherworld now that he had passed over. It seemed that every Chicago matron who came to the tea room lately was positive Rudy had been attempting to contact them. Reba had become very adroit at indulging her customer's fantasies, especially with the promising rewards of fat tips that would always follow favorable readings. It was easy to read a blank mind with insipid thoughts curling around the edges.

Young Valentino's tragic death had been her second personal tragedy. Two months previously, on August 23rd, the terrible day he had passed over, Reba felt she had lost her ethereal lover, her beloved sheik, her soul mate. When she read the morning newspapers the following day after his death, she had left work early, tips or no tips, that afternoon. She had unleashed a torrent of tears through the rest of the day and into late evening, while leafing through a bulging scrapbook filled with Valentino clippings from movie magazines and newspapers. For sustenance during this tragic period, actually that day, she had devoured three boxes of double-dipped, chocolate covered cherries which later had given her the runs for two days and troubled dreams during the night.

Every theater on State Street and in the Loop had shown his movies; special edition newspapers rendered lurid accounts of his premature and admittedly, rather suspicious death. Now, two months later, the customers in the tea room continued to pack every booth and private VIP room, wanting special Valentino readings from cards and tea leaves, and Reba, being as shrewd as she was, went for the tips instead of wasting time in sympathetic cooing.

Her fanciful readings on Valentino had attracted a steady gaggle of morbidly curious matrons and their daughters.

At times, the demand for personal requests was more than she could handle. On several occasions she had nearly broken down in tears, upset with sexual message requests and rather intimate poems the ladies wanted her to relay to her Valentino.

Reba deeply sighed again with thoughts of Peter and memories of Valentino, and after blowing her nose in a well-worn dainty Irish linen handkerchief, rose from the kitchen table and walked to the small shabby bedroom, where she sat down in front of a dust covered vanity mirror.

Slowly she raked a comb through her dyed, bobbed black hair, her lone concession to fashion. She skillfully applied a splotch of bright red rouge to her pale cheeks, followed by a heavily lip-sticked cupid's bow to her thin lips, pausing a minute to glance at the green velvet-framed wedding picture of Peter and herself, and she remembered.

Peter was a good looker, filled with the vibrant life juices of passion and exceptional love. Those memories continued to leave her breathless and hot around the neck and bosom, especially in remembering Friday's weekly baths. Reba's deceased parents had not been happy with her marriage to that "Big, dumb Polish ox," but then they had not known what a gentle and loving man he had been.

They had met at the neighborhood Polish Catholic church, St. Catherine's, where she had been a volunteer cook and server for the neighborhood destitute. Peter had been working as a handy man for the parish hall and church, and was strongly considering going to an upstate Illinois seminary for the priesthood. He had been waiting for acceptance by the Chicago Archdiocese until he met Reba.

Peter was a traumatized war veteran, still shocked over what he had seen and experienced in France's trenches during the Great War, and like many other veterans of that war, he would never be emotionally whole again. He had wandered from coast to coast for several years, dangerously riding the rails, never feeling he would find the glue to stick to any place and settle down.

Finally tap-rooting somewhat in south-side Chicago, Peter returned to his Polish Catholic faith, and with encouragement from the parish priests, decided to enter the protection of the priesthood. That was, until he met the big-breasted woman who smothered him in her arms and helped him rediscover his manhood.

Six months after they had met they married in a white-hot heat of lust that never seemed to chill. No children came from this union because they both felt that kids and responsibility would dilute their passion; actually, his reason was because of war memories and death, and Reba's was her controlling parents. They never had any regrets over this decision.

Tears again pooled in the corners of her eyes. She went to the scarred Maple chest of drawers, pulled out the top drawer seeking another handkerchief. Reba's hazel eyes immediately locked onto the silver-framed, autographed black and white glossy photograph of Rudolph Valentino rakishly dressed in a white Arab burnoose. His smoldering dark eyes and sensuously pursed lips never failed to send lustful chills through out her body. The clerk in the Loop gift shop had insisted it was Valentino's genuine signature and accordingly was expensive, costing Reba three days worth of tips.

Her lips tightened while tears streamed down her cheeks, snaking abstract patterns of salt-water rivulets through ivory face powder, rouge and mascara. She washed her face in the rusted bathroom sink, and again sat down at the vanity mirror to reapply makeup to her puffy, bloodless face.

Reba made her way into the central smoke-filled tea room, mildly surprised over the milling crowd positioning for tables in the private rooms. She speculated that it would be another pain-in-the-ass-day filled with demanding socialites. Several smartly dressed women in skirts and dresses, hem lines inches above their knees, clothes that only their Flapper daughters should wear, smiled with her entrance. She heard two voices acknowledging her appearance.

"That's her. Now, Dora, we mustn't have any other reader but her. You'll see what I mean when she does our readings!"

Another voice, languid and bitchy replied, "Do you really believe she's in contact with the dead?"

"Just wait, you'll see!"

Reba knew she was late again, but instead of fretting, smiled at the thought of Chicago's richest grand dames waiting for the likes of her. She knew she was now the main draw of the tea room, if not, then the old dragon, Madame Rossi, would've thrown her butt out in the street long ago.

"You naughty girl, we've been waiting for you!"

Madame Rossi stood a few feet from her, internally debating a confrontation with Reba while absent mindedly twisting an opera length necklace of garnet beads with short sausage-fat fingers.

"Mrs. Palmerston and her two darling daughters are waiting for you in the Romanoff Room. Your smock is hanging on the clothes hook." The razor-sharp tone in her voice indicated haste.

Without a word, Reba quick-stepped to the largest VIP room, pulled on the crisply starched, black smock edged with what passed for lace, flying dramatically into the room. She knew she could spend only 20 minutes per group or with a single customer for the required fast turnover.

She swirled Mrs. Palmerston's now emptied tea cup, turning it upside down over the saucer with a quick flick of her wrist. She focused her thoughts while she willed the tea leaves to form abstract patterns in the cup and saucer. She gazed deeply for effect into the clotted leaves for additional mentally counted seconds.

"Well, Mrs. Palmerston, I see that one of your daughters will soon be meeting--this very spring I believe, the man she will marry. He seems to be highly connected in New York society--is very wealthy...a partner in a top drawer law firm, I'm sure of it."

Before she could continue, the oldest daughter, Lennore, burst out, "It's William! I told you it was going to be him. I'm so excited! I knew it was going to happen!" She almost swooned.

"Well, Miss Woolzaki, as usual, you're right on the mark."

Reba did not correct the mangling of her name. Generous tips had taught her long ago to hold her tongue.

She was bone-tired by seven that evening when the tea room closed. It was getting increasingly difficult to handle the mob that waited daily for tea readings and the occasional Tarot.

After Reba pulled her smock off and had stuffed eleven dollars and change from tips into a shoddy hand bag, Madame Rossi cornered her in the VIP room while she was clearing the table. Reba groaned, wondering if she was going to get chastised over having been late after all. She was surprised.

"My dear, a special request--I was asked by "the" Mrs. Bolton, for your attendance at a special séance tomorrow night, which will be held at her city house on the lake. Dr. Wolverton, the founder of the Chicago Spiritualist Study Society, has heard about you, and is strongly hoping that you will participate as the main sitter at this séance."

Reba could only summon exhaustion and resentment.

"My dear Reba, this is a great honor for you, and of course our tea room. Chicago society doesn't just ask "anybody" to come into their grand mansions--especially "The" Mrs. Wendell Bolton...Please, just for me, this time?"

Reba also knew this command put her continued employment at the tea room on the line if she refused. Mrs. Rossi had a tendency to shoot herself in the foot, especially when her sudden mood swings turned into raging bitch sessions; several times during these moody episodes she had dismissed good readers on a heated whim.

Reba was stunned at the magnificent gray-stone castle residence sprawling for several acres on Lake Michigan's Gold Coast. The pasty-faced butler carefully scrutinized her, obvious disdain written across his pointed little face. He helped her remove her rag-tag cloth coat, holding it away from his body as if it contained fleas, while leading her to the massive room which passed for an intimate French salon, located off the black and white marble parquet-floored entry hall way, she had entered from the front doors.

When she saw the four fashion-plate dressed matrons and Dr. Wolverton, who was posing by the blazing fireplace in an expensively tailored tuxedo, Reba suddenly grew furious. Furious over being in the lavish Bolton mansion--the same family which owned the railroad that had fought her meager widow's pension. She knew they didn't know, nor would they even care if they knew about Peter's tragic death. Reba mentally dropped to a low boiling point she had to force herself into for defusing this anger; it was going to be hard, but what little status or influence she had accrued these past months, could be lost in a minute's explosion.

After a lengthy introduction by Dr. Wolverton of his credentials and brief introductions of the elegantly dressed matrons, Reba was seated near the massive French Gothic fireplace, where roaring flames licked out at the intrusion of a nobody, in the presence of the some bodies.

Dr. Wolverton seemed to smirk as he spoke:

"Miss. Walizuski, we are assembled for contact with the spirit force of Rudolph Valentino. Mrs. Bolton feels that you might be the Medium that will enable us to make contact with him from the other side."

Reba winced. Valentino again! She promptly decided not to get upset over this personal invasion into the affairs of her sheik because she needed the sixty dollar fee. She bit her lip.

He continued prattling on, while obviously doubting her abilities.

"I understand as a Sensitive, that you have had some interesting successes in these spiritual matters of contact."

Reba nodded. She did not want to be shown-up, feeling that Madame Rossi's instructions in Mediumship was probably as good as anything Dr. Wolverton could ever summon up, or she wouldn't be here. As a matter of fact, she rather enjoyed being the center of attention. And, she had seen the departed since she was a little girl—and had also talked to them. She had never been afraid of spirits.

She knew, since she was about twelve years old, that she had this special "gift". Her mother and father frequently dragged her to the priests at St. Catherine's to dispel this evil phase she obviously was going through; she was properly contrite when the angry priests would browbeat her, but she was always sure that they knew she was not to be meddled with. She had been confused by her mother and father's vehemence when it came to using these gifts because they admitted to her that they were able to exercise these abilities also.

She was confused by this confession until she grew much older.

But, Reba was unable to contact her beloved Peter. She had never attempted to contact her prince, Valentino, sure that when he was ready, he would contact her. She sighed again.

When they were seated, Dr. Wolverton looked around the table: "Remember ladies, no discussions or movements are allowed during the sitting. Agreed?"

He again looked through Reba as if she was something from the bottom of his shoe, doubt etched across his face. "Wilton, please turn out the lights, the light from the fireplace will be more than sufficient."

On Wolverton's cue, the nervous sitters put their hands palm down on the table, each touching the hands of the participants to their sides in order to insure a connected circle of energy and protection, the magical ancient circle of hands.

Reba spoke nervously, "I'm ready."

She cleared her mind while mentally visualizing the photograph of Valentino sitting on her bedroom chest of drawers. Minutes passed before she slipped into trance, the only sound in the darkened room coming from the cracking and popping of burning logs in the gigantic French Gothic fireplace.

Reba felt a sudden swirl of cold air enveloping her. Instantly, goose bumps rose on the back of her neck and her chubby arms. She knew the spiritual door to the other side was opening.

"Rudy, our dear sweet prince, we desire to contact you... beloved Rudolph Valentino, please come to us."

She felt strange, having no control over why she spoke those words--they seemed to tumble through her mind, then forcefully spilled from her mouth. Reba felt nauseated over being controlled.

Cool air and a strange feeling permeated the room, the air swirling more noticeably now, intensifying into a cold and dank draft which seemed to attack every corner of the room. Flickering tongues of flames from the fireplace seemed to reach out into the dark room with the increased volume of the draft.

Then she saw "It." Reba gasped, enough to cause the sitters around the table to gasp in unison over the shock. She was surprised at its appearance and stunned that she had actually been able to summon an entity. Could it really be him?

Her disbelieving eyes strained with exertion while focusing on the gauzy, transparent, somehow white entity suspended above the table. She glanced momentarily at the mute figures sitting around the table, observing faces frozen in horrified shock. The salon was filled with pungent smells of must, heady mildew...and the odor of an embalmed funeral parlor corpse.

The spector blurred at first then became a slowly emerging form--from a one dimensional apparition turning into a solid materialization. "It" was, or once was, a human male, less than six feet tall, naked and seemingly coated in some sort of a sickly shade of green-white, misty-like substance.

Yes, it was him! Reba's heart beat frantically and she gulped for air. The spirit of Valentino attempted speech, his mouth opening and closing rapidly like a gasping fish out of water; his hands fluttered to his throat, squeezing the words from his mouth.

The accented voice came in several minutes, reed-thin at first, then forced and low timbered.

"Reba, what do you want?"

She barely restrained herself from jumping out of the chair when her name was spoken, finding her throat paralyzed in fear. She forced herself to speak. The prince of love knew her name!

Reba's quivering voice managed to squeak out an acknowledgment,

"We miss you Rudy, your passing still pains us--

you can't be gone, not from the ones who love you so much!"

In a heavily accented Italian voice, the spirit spoke while looking around the room, "Why don't you silly fools let me rest in peace! I thought I was done with your stupid world, now you drag me back!"

With these words, Mrs. Bolton groaned, falling to the floor face down, buried under her overturned chair. Mrs. Landry Phillips jumped out of her chair, intending a quick leap to the closed door. A low, guttural voice ripped through the fear-choked room. The other three women and Dr. Wolverton continued to stare at the apparition in shock.

"You--stay where you are! All of you! I'm not finished."

Mrs. Phillips sat down, her eye balls rolling upward in fright, the pearl whites of her eyes revealing terror and an oncoming seizure.

The spirit continued, "It takes a long time for the soul to realize the body's shell is empty, and this shock is the worst thing you'll ever go through. I wanted sleep, now you have closed that door to my transition with this silly parlor game. This is an insult to me and a very dangerous path for you to take, dear Reba, you should have known better!"

Valentino's apparition drew closer to Reba.

His nose flared as he spat at her, "You have strong powers, cara mia! I won't forget this moment with you, perhaps I will never forgive you for this boorishness. A parlor game, indeed! I might even stay with you and yours for a very long time. You do love me, don't you Reba? Well, I might indeed love you to death!"

He tugged at his wrist, pulled hard, throwing an object at her.

The shock of Valentino's appearance finally became too much for Reba. She fainted, her head falling forward on the massive oak table with a loud clunk.

Moments later she woke with a throbbing headache and rivulets of foaming spittle running down her chin onto her ample bosom. She looked around the table, finding terror etched into the faces of the sitters. Mrs. Bolton was still on the floor, the upturned chair covering her unconscious body. Dr. Wolverton's eyes were opened wide in death, his hands frozen in a vise grip on his starched shirt front. The others were sitting in horrified, catatonic postures, very much afraid of leaving their chairs.

Reba was in a state of denial over what she had seen and her mind worked furiously to cancel the reality of what had just happened. She noticed a gleaming object a few inches from her on the table. A gold bracelet! She scooped it up in her trembling hands and dropped it down her bodice, not once wondering why Valentino had thrown it at her. It was obviously a love offering given to her from her sheik.

She vomited on the table from excitement and fear.

Chapter 1

DENVER, 2011

Emma Glass sat cat-still while peering into a gilded antique vanity mirror. The room was crypt-quiet except for sporadic morning birdsong that penetrated the bedroom cloister through open French doors. The bird chirps that managed to interrupt the sanctity of stillness came riding into the room on gusts of dry winds, hurled from a roaring down-draft in the steep Colorado foothills.

The combination of wind and birdsong snapped Emma's reverie, causing her to break away from the worn diamond-dust backed mirror. She wasn't vain, far from it. Lately, it had become an easy meditational escape to sit at the Louis XVI vanity table while brushing her hair, an early morning ritual of release, and a feeble attempt at temporarily silencing the mind chatter which brought the damnable headaches and migraines that almost crippled her.

Faint voices, like several people whispering in an echoing hall, faint enough to be word indistinguishable, usually preceded the announcement of the migraines. If she had been of a weaker disposition she was positive these voices would have thrown her to her knees and perhaps worse, driven her over the edge. Yes, she still had control, but at times she was also convinced that had she been a weaker wreck, then they would have taken control of her being. They were also growing in strength—it would be difficult to beat them back.

Emma could never tell anyone about these voices, afraid of additional therapy sessions; by acknowledging these voices, she would give them recognition, hence, power of materialization and release into the world. But none the less, these very real forces would have to be dealt with down the road. Of course she had believed that no matter how stable or educated an individual was, personal demons were with all of us.

She grew listless while staring deeply into the now cloudy mirror, anticipating relief from morose thoughts of depression. During these fits of frustration and depression she would enter into a hypnotic state, and if she focused hard, she was able to free her mind from time and all surroundings—a total zoning out from unpleasant reality incidents, her therapist had said. Whatever it was, Emma came to welcome these stolen interludes because they banished her cluster migraines leaving her feeling refreshed and at peace. Emma's occasional use of medications also helped, but never as much as her ability to enter into trance, that marvelous ability which blocked out everything hurtful she had to deal with thanks to a local recreation center Zen course coupled with a week meditation retreat in Vail.

Her radiant complexion was flawless except for slight sinus pouches that hung beneath her sea-green eyes. She reached for a brown frosted glass bottle of makeup, shaking the small bottle several times, uncapping it and skillfully applying the moist contents under her eyes.

Struggling with persistent depression over turning thirty-eight three weeks ago and suffering from feelings of stress and sleeplessness, Emma felt justified in using any kind of makeup, knowing she looked good on the outside. Inside was another story she couldn't put to rest.

Emma gave a cursory once over glance at her mirrored reflection, not wanting the discovery of new laugh lines or crow's feet. Satisfied that she was somewhat eluding time, she again picked up the heavy Georgian silver brush from the vanity table and gently administered even strokes through her neck length, lustrous auburn hair. She had been told that she was a drop-dead beauty, but a melange of festering insecurities had given her too many doubts as to what others really perceived her to be.

One of the numerous self-help books she had half read said that who you are lies beyond your material body. Absurd, she thought, but it stuck with her, like another pick-up sentence from yet another half read, Oprah self-help book Emma had remembered, one passage empirically stating that all endings are merely new beginnings and opportunities. Trite to be sure, then mulled these thoughts over again while continuing to brush her gray-free hair. She also loved the simple quick Zen snippets and koans she could recall when she needed to steady herself.

Stopping in mid-stroke from brushing she stared deeply into her reflection, sometimes feeling trapped in the mirror and finding it difficult to break the intense spells that came out of nowhere. She had found herself in this state frequently the past few weeks, feeling guilty that she dwelled on herself far too much and too often lately. Emma also knew, or at least felt strongly, that big changes were about to enter into her life. And some misgivings again swept into her subconscious. She hoped that this increasingly neurotic behavior was not going to push her into another breakdown. She shuddered with that thought.

The therapist had administered intensive counseling sessions during back to back sessions, no holds barred, and never quite strong enough to exorcise the depression that hovered in the lonely shadows of her mind, especially at night, which even now seemed to grow in menace and intensity during the day. She refused to take medication when alone, actually very seldom now, telling the therapist she was tired of taking "nut pills," as she called them, neurotically afraid of becoming dependent on drugs, choosing instead to master anxiety episodes with self-control. She filled the prescriptions dutifully and as soon as she reached home, threw them in the trash after saving a small amount in case she suffered a "ragged" episode.

Two years ago, on a blustery, early spring Sunday afternoon, Emma's carefully constructed world had been shattered by a terse telephone call from the Colorado Highway Patrol: her husband Travis, and his best friend Willie Garza, had suddenly vanished under a snow slide near the Copper Mountain Resort while cross country skiing in a restricted area prone to avalanches. After an intense search that lasted three days, under the worst of blizzard conditions, their bodies buried deeply under unforgiving snow, were never found. Even when the snow melted, retreating under the warming sun of an early Colorado spring, the mountains refused to surrender the men's remains.

The memorial service for both professors had been held at the Evans Chapel on the campus of Denver University four weeks later. Emma could not recall one minute of the never ending service, only the minister's concluding remarks, "Life is like grabbing water," which joined the mish-mash of other random quotes she pondered on from her daily journal, especially reading when she felt vulnerable and frazzled.

Strangely, Emma could vividly recall the overflow crowd of mourners, how they were dressed, even the exact words of their personal condolences. When she and Willie's wife, Jana, had made their way to the chapel's parking lot after the service, they'd been forced to stop several times while being surrounded, touched and hugged by faceless people, frozen memory bites that would forever remind her of the classical Greek tragedies she had once loved so fervently.

Emma would never be able to erase that surrealistic day from her memory, a slow motion drama stolen from the Swedish film maker, Ingmar Bergman. She felt the bleak, noir day had been ordered for Bergman's direction: cold, gray sleeting snow, chills and depression, and a wall of faceless people dressed in black. She felt this late insulting spring snow storm had been the perfect setting for a final farewell, a farewell kiss from nature announcing Emma's starring role as a pathetic, untouchable widow. She knew she could not, would not, ever fall in love again in the same way she had with Travis. Travis had been that special man who loved and cherished women, the only male she had ever permitted herself to share honest, emotional intimacies with. For the past two years she had fleetingly thought of that memorial service, especially when her defenses were dropped and she was weak and needy; the shadowy faces never seemed to come into focus, but she still felt they were observing her, waiting to see if she would fail. The therapist had said these faceless people represented society in general, how she viewed most people as being nameless and faceless entities, all indicating a withdrawal and detachment from her environment and close human contact.

In these weakened situations she conjured up memories of Princess Diana. She felt a tight bond with this Woman-Goddess, who was beyond beautiful, was coy, desirable, having a mind of her own. Like Emma she had been abused—no, used, as in Diana's case as a broodmare, then thrown into the woods by her Prince for a tart. However, Diana refused to quit and fade into the shadows of nondescript wallpaper for palace convenience, instead, becoming even more beautiful, sophisticated and loved across the world--even without her prince charming. No matter, Diana wasn't perfect, as most women spurned were not allowed to be independent and free thinkers.

Emma remembered Diana's wedding, the birth of the boys, being ignored, and her elevation to the most wonderful princess in the world--every girl's dream; then the days of death, tears and horror from the aftermath of a very strange auto accident--just like Emma's parents.

The personal feelings Emma garnered from the saga of Princess Diana was, that if you wanted to let it happen, or allowed it to happen, then she too could become a victim. Emma was still very much alive and was fighting her unwilling assignment as widow, and the unwanted title of childless matron.

A university widow's pension, two large insurance polices, several lucrative investment portfolios, along with three owned houses, an exceptional modern art collection on temporary loan to the Denver and Chicago Art Museums, and several world-wide bank accounts, including two special off-shore accounts-- all had guaranteed a more than comfortable standard of living set up for the recent wealthy widow.

This income however, did not give her what she desperately needed, a second chance to be cherished. Although Travis had left her well-heeled, he also had left her very much alone and vulnerable, loving her much too well, the water mark of this perceived perception she felt, would be impossible to ever be found again.

His death had been a bitter shock of what she felt life was really about—Russian Roulette, a hit and miss reality. Emma no longer had Travis as a buffer. His death ended their popular parties, joint cooking of gourmet dinners, late night intimate conversations, the excitement of discovering new mountain hiking paths and cycling trails, camping, world travel, love, exciting sex, and the intimacy of just being together.

Travis Glass had found the cave of depression Emma had been held hostage in, and together they had joined forces at confronting the dragon that refused to release her.

Emma had been sexually abused in several of the countless foster homes she had been briefly dumped in, and then just as quickly ripped out by the Cook County Department of Social Services. When she became eighteen and emancipated, she matriculated to Chicago University. Her facade of detachment from social interaction caged her in isolation. Her coolness and hostility not only rebuffed, it created a deep canyon of separation from her peer group.

She had easily obtained a three year Bachelor's Degree at Chicago University laced with honors achieved by taking a grinding overload of subjects, and by going to school through the summer semesters. It was not a perversion in Emma's character that had made her live a lonely life through academics, it was her only life and an escape from a world that she felt had rejected her.

Her wealthy parents had given Emma carte blanch for life's options through an enormous trust fund activated after their untimely death in a freak road accident—a very strange auto accident. She never had to draw down on the trust during her college years because of her scholarships.

The entire estate had gone to Emma on her twenty-first birthday without any objections or claims, as she had no living or contesting relatives, not even kissing cousins were known. The firm of lawyers that had managed the estate never once had come up with a single conservator or custodian to alleviate her bleak childhood, so she had ended up as a wealthy ward of the state of Illinois, living below the state poverty line simply because nobody in authority would take any initiative.

Emma's first action at age twenty-one was to ensure that every penny in her trust fund had been accounted for. She did this by hiring an expensive CPA firm over the hearty objections of the law firm. This accounting inquiry bottom-lined at $3,967,000 on hand, plus considerable interest for "accidentally misplaced" funds. She had hoped the law firm would balk or refute the large sum of money owed to her estate, thus giving her the chance to sue and humiliate the firm that had deserted her in childhood, but they hadn't.

She was amazed at the huge sum of money left to her from her parents because she never remembered that they had been rich. At all. She obviously had been much too young to understand it anyway.

Emma had found an estate planning and investment agent through a random e-mail message via an Internet search over the strong objections of the law firm. This Internet relationship proved to be very lucrative through the years for both Emma and the investment agent. She also never asked why the large sums of interest seemed to grow so fast and to be so much, even during downturns in the economy.

A second action occurred when she reached her majority. She was able to seduce a young Doctoral candidate she had observed in the reference section of the Chicago University library. She was attracted to him when she felt, for the very first time in her life, lust surging in her privates that she had never experienced before, wondering what sex with him would be like.

Emma briefly met Bill Garnet while he was a teacher's assistant in one of her Russian classes; he had been thoroughly amazed with her knowledge of Russian history and language, and Emma was impressed with his scholarly research in Russian history and language. Her plan for his total seduction was birthed from that moment. She became even more taken with his quick wit and daily devotion to running six miles and working out in the college gym. She had been impressed with his exceptional mind lodged in a perfect body—the classical Greek ideal.

She thought Garnet was the most physically beautiful male she had ever seen, and since he seemed to be interested in her, she eventually allowed him to take her "new" virginity—her sexual abuse in the foster homes hadn't really taken her virginity she reasoned, because it hadn't been given willingly.

The path of her seduction had been carefully planned: she flirted, bought him gifts, laughed at his inane jokes, frequently rubbed against him, making it very apparent that she would be an easy conquest.

They shared numerous liaisons in an unused library office deep in the basement stacks, at her apartment, motels which she paid for, and in the showers at an old, seldom used university faculty gym after finishing their daily early morning runs.

The affair lasted nearly seven months until seeing him one day at the Lincoln Park Zoo with his wife and small son, his family, which he had neglected to tell her about. It gave her the easy out she had been looking for. Except for the rutting rabbit sex, Emma never once was upset from their break-up after the confrontation, actually rather relived that their fling was over with. She got what she had wanted from the relationship: curiosity satisfied about sex, the willing loss of her "virginity," and the thrill of seducing a man. She felt triumphant about acquiring this worldly knowledge, feeling the exciting tingle of being a jaded, loose woman, especially elated when he begged her to resume their affair while trembling with tears in his eyes. Her tingles continued to grow—she was triumphant!

Several academic honors and a Phi Beta Kappa key for a 4.4 average attracted a full-grant scholarship, leading to a quick Master's degree in Anthropology at Northwestern. After she obtained her Masters' she was accepted as a doctoral candidate at Denver University. There she had met and married Travis Glass.

Travis was intellectual, gregarious, adventurous and a fanatical outdoors man. He was gentle, self-effacing and imbued with a great amount of fortitude--a suitor who had made it his mission to snare a bitter Emma Lyon Benton into marriage.

It had taken Travis Glass over a year of intense and aggressive courtship mixed with gentle coaxing to entice Emma into dating, sex, and eventually into marriage. When he had finally probed deep enough through her mental fortress he discovered a brilliant, strong-willed younger woman who had never trusted any man since she had been nine years old.

When he had uncovered the deeply buried secrets of sexual abuse, he carefully peeled her armor away like flower petals, one at a time. When Emma reached the decision to trust, she had fallen hopelessly in love for the very first time in her life. All barriers and doubts collapsed at once when she had surrendered to this persistent suitor.

A small Denver society wedding at the Brown Palace Hotel and a six week honeymoon of unfettered sex, sun, and sailing at the Glass family, tax-dodge Bermuda villa, laid the cornerstone of their husband and wife partnership. She was twenty-three years old, he was twenty-five, and they were deeply in love.

Through their thirteen years of marriage, they both had become associate professors at Denver University, he in psychology, she in anthropology. Emma was quickly inducted into the social network of university and Denver society. Her newly found wit, energy and charm, enhanced by Travis's family name and old money were the decided pluses for entry through tightly closed doors.

The children they both desperately wanted never

came, with four miscarriages. Extensive tests from the Mayo Clinic were inconclusive. Emma was far more upset than Travis over not having children, inwardly sure that the years of sexual abuse she had undergone as a child was a pay-back from a painful past, regardless if she had nothing to do with what happened. She felt guilty that she had somehow been to blame for attracting the negatives that seemed to cling to her like a magnet.

Emma fumbled through a green leather jewelry box looking for an accent piece to compliment the one piece black dress she was wearing. She found a heavy, antique gold bracelet that had belonged to her grandmother Tonopolski, the links which Emma had shortened over the jeweler's protest in order to fit her small wrist. She had saved the excess links.

She fished through the vanity drawer, finding the black velvet box containing the gold necklace coiled with small, brilliant square-cut emeralds, the specially commissioned necklace Travis had given her for their thirteenth wedding anniversary. Tears pooled in her eyes while she stroked the necklace, vividly recalling the night of the gift all too well. She hurriedly placed it back in the velvet box, slamming the drawer shut.

She still couldn't wear "his" necklace, the memory of the anniversary celebration with a house-full of their dearest friends at a surprise dinner party, still pained when remembered. She'd even removed the oil painting from the bedroom fireplace which depicted them in the clothes they had worn that night; the painting had been her belated gift to him.

Emma was late again. She whipped the silver gray BMW north on University Boulevard, and then sharply screeched left into the driveway of the Hampden Club.

The restaurant's interior was layered in chiaroscuro shadows despite a bright, early afternoon sunlight that sliced through the finger-smudged, diamond-paned windows and French doors. The eye was immediately drawn to huge windows at the end of the long, dark entryway, overlooking a small algae-flecked lake and well manicured golf course.

No host met her at the entry hall of the restaurant, forcing her to carefully search her way across the uneven flagstones of the entryway, and through the cloistered shadows of the central dining room, searching each dimly lit red leather booth for her best friend.

She found Donna at the last table near the south French doors. Donna Epstein glanced up from an enormous tasseled menu with a look of feigned surprise.

"I thought I was going to be stood up again."

"Please forgive me for missing yesterday. My head is still a mess...migraines again."

Donna patted Emma's hand in sympathy while she was sitting down. "I understand. You poor dear." Donna meant it.

Emma hated mentioning anything concerning her health, always afraid of openly displaying any kind of vulnerability, but Donna knew so much about her that she had long ago discarded any barrier.

"What's the special today?"

"Crab cakes, or fish mousse, Salmon I think, or something disgusting like that. The soup of the day is Clam Chowder. I'm going to order a small New York cut and a mixed green salad."

"Sounds good. Me too."

Donna poured Emma a glass of red wine, Donna's favorite imported French Merlot, from a cut-glass carafe while Emma watched.

Emma turned her cell phone off and looked at Donna, hoping that she would do the same. Between both of them, their cell phones could easily disrupt their time together, and could even bring Charles, the manager of the club to their table.

Donna's wrist jangled with a hoard of diamond studded bracelets as she poured wine into Emma's glass. Emma quickly appraised Donna: a designer, one piece forest green dress that clung tightly to her lithe figure; every chic black hair in place, a delicate, wrinkle free face that begged a portrait by a master painter, in other words, Donna was a diminutive beauty that time belied forty-four years. Wealth did have its advantages when doing battle with the years.

They had met at a Yoga studio four years ago and found out they had several things in common: travel, reading, good food and charity work. Donna had been between husbands and needed the release of exercise and meditation to get back into the hunt of looking for husband number four. Donna had a quick, sardonic wit that had immediately attracted Emma.

"You look wonderful as usual; black is definitely your color." Donna could have bitten her lip.

Emma blanched at the slip, almost making a wise crack to let Donna off the hook, then decided to let it go. She preferred wearing mourning black or navy blue ever since Travis's death.

Donna Epstein had been her best friend for four years. They trusted each other, so much so that they knew each others' deepest secrets, and they never intentionally hurt each others' feelings, hence black and the reference to death, the inference of a widow, which was quickly forgotten.

"How's Tom? I'm not prying, but I feel a marriage or something is about to erupt. Am I right?" She had a smirk on her beautiful face.

It took the wind out of Emma's sails for a few seconds. Donna never missed speaking her mind.

"No, nothing like that. She blushed. He's been my rudder, really good for me...after Travis's death... oh, you know what I mean!" She felt like a silly adolescent.

"Honey, I know he looks a little like Travis, as a matter of fact they could be bookends, naturally being brothers and all, but do you really think you're being fair to him?"

"Hell, I don't know. He's a beautiful man, and when we're together I feel like I'm with Travis. God, is that sick or what? And I do love him Donna, just not in the same way I loved Travis."

"I'm not a shrink. You'll have to let go of Travis eventually--it just isn't good for your mental health." She patted Emma on the hand again and continued,

VALENTINO'S CURSE

"I guess when its right you'll know it, God only knows, I wish I had a man with hot looks, muscles and money that was bedding me—God, he even has brains." They both laughed, Emma blushing.

They ate while making light conversation. Donna looked at Emma.

"That bracelet is a beauty, new?"

Emma looked at it, and then undid the safety clasp handing it to Donna. "No, it's not new."

"I just love gold, especially when it's so heavy, this could break a wrist. This must have cost a small fortune—I'm sure it's at least 22 Karats, did Travis give it to you?"

"It was my grandmother's, I think. I'm not sure, I was too young, but I think my mother said it had once belonged to a silent movie star from the twenties, Valentino...yes, that's who--Rudolph Valentino. It was some sort of gift. Mother told me a story about it, but I can't remember. She would never wear it, claiming it was cursed—whatever, something silly like that. I carried it around to the foster homes I was in and almost lost it several times, but I managed to hang on to it amazingly. I'm sure people thought it was costume jewelry."

"His! Wow, just think Em, 'the' Valentino! Quite a guy. I saw an old silent movie on Public television in which he was an Arab sheik, or the son of a sheik, something like that...wasn't very old when he died."

They almost finished another carafe of wine, growing tipsy with the comfort of friendship and conversation and the added heat of the early afternoon.

After Donna paid the bill they made their way to the parking lot. Emma was growing morose, thinking about how she would be spending another lonely night at home after another pointless afternoon of shopping for something she didn't need, at the Cherry Creek Mall. Tom was in Aspen for a five day health conference.

She fought asking Donna to spend the night at her house, and quickly decided not to go shopping. She was wondering if she should renew her Yoga membership at the studio because it would help to fill the empty hours of restlessness, perhaps even taking her mind off manufactured angst.

"May I borrow Valentino's alleged bracelet for tonight? I'm going to my Mediumship study group, the one where we have spiritual enfolding--correction, spiritual unfoldment training, and the Medium, Karl Michael, is instructing us on how to develop skill in Psychometry, um, getting vibrations from objects. It's supposed to be really accurate. I promise I'll take good care of this bauble. It would be so much fun if it really was his!"

Emma fumbled with the heavy duty latch clasp, finally handing it to Donna, her mind still on another lonely night ahead. She didn't mean to, but she was really bored with Donna's constant chatter. She decided to drive straight home instead of mall shopping, have tea and work in the garden till dark.

Chapter 2

Emma carried a tray of freshly brewed tea and a carrot-raisin muffin to the huge master bedroom with the dark corners. She hunted through the bedroom several minutes looking for the book she had been reading on the archaeology of southern Colorado's Crow Canon. She pushed a CD of James Taylor into the stereo and commenced reading the book in the day bed.

She sighed deeply, the rose gardens had been perfect, not requiring her attention. She had been a creature of habit for several years. Molly-Kathleen, her beloved Rhodesian Ridgeback, used to be her very close companion and soul mate, especially filling in the hours when Travis had taught late classes or chaired never ending faculty meetings.

Emma would take long walks with her powerful protector through the park next to their house while she listened on the I-pod to her favorite rock group, the Rolling Stones. Whenever she heard their recording of 'You can't always get what you want,' she would think of the park walks. Molly, her shadow, had died two months after Travis's death, Emma sure she had died from a broken heart. Emma never wanted another dog, knowing it would be impossible to recreate another personality like her close friend.

The telephone rang. Reaching for the telephone she noticed that the Waterford clock read 10:50. She thought it might be Tom calling from Aspen; it was Donna in rapid fire.

"Well, guess what? The Valentino bracelet. It scared the shit out of Karl. He started choking, then threw it across the room like he'd been bitten. It didn't break or anything, but my god, I've never seen a man jump that high from a sitting position. Well, it boils down to this...would you be available tomorrow night? Honey, please don't say no. He wants you to join our little study circle, as a matter of fact, he says that you must come. Before you object--please, for me? Pretty please! I'm going to be destroyed if you don't come, and yes, I know how you feel about this stuff."

Emma was surprised at how quickly she had given in. She agreed only because she did not want to spend another evening alone. It was lonely in the house without Tom.

The Church of Divine Harmony was surprisingly large. Emma was convinced the séance study circle would be held in some small sleazy building or in the basement of somebody's house. The church was built of red flagstone and was prosperous looking, even having the feel of a real church. The vast expanse of lawn and evergreen shrubs was superbly manicured, which to her had always been an indication that a family, business, or an organization was respectable.

Karl Michael and his assistant, Jack Sewell were in their early forties, much too slender for tall men, both well groomed, and somehow, in some way-- strange. Sewell spoke with a slight English accent that always hinted at exhaustion.

Michael spoke to her in a conspiratorial tone. "Thank you for coming Emma, eh, may I call you Emma?" Not waiting for approval he continued, "You don't know how important this séance will be to us, maybe all of us. I think you'll find the evening to be most interesting, possibly enough to open another door for life's spiritual journey." He paused, mulling over what he had just spoken, "Sorry, I'm always recruiting."

VALENTINO'S CURSE

With the pause that followed his comment, Donna squeezed Emma's arm for a please-do-not-make-a-comment rebuttal.

Emma and Donna were escorted into a small waiting room by Sewell, and as soon as he left, Donna tore through her purse seeking a package of cigarettes.

"Found it, care for one?"

"I don't think so. No...not now."

While Donna lit her cigarette Emma quickly scanned the small room. Comfortable, she thought, a quasi attempt at English country decor, properly sedate and underscored with money.

"This church...eh, temple, must do pretty well."

Donna looked at Emma. "Oh yes, we do quite well."

"We?"

"I am an active member, you know. Ever since my father died I've belonged. You remember what a mess I was going through? With the divorce from Josh, then Dad's death--well, the strain was too much. I can still recall the night I changed for good—vividly!"

She stared at Emma intently while she continued to speak.

"It was snowing, I was drunk, I had just left the

Red Ribbon Bar and almost landed in Cherry Creek, you know, near Colorado Boulevard and Speer. Well, my dear, I was in shock. I was out of my damn mind, crying--crying hell, I was damn hysterical, and then he came!" Donna paused, but this time it was not for dramatic effect.

Emma swallowed hard while she looked deeply into Donna's unblinking blue eyes. She knew part of the incident, but now she was going to hear the rest, something that would be very unsettling she was sure.

"Who came?"

"Daddy. He was sitting in the car, right next to me in the passenger seat. I could smell his favorite cologne, 'Top Deck'. Damn it, he touched me, then patted my hand. I couldn't talk! Not a squeak! He then said, 'Sweet heart, you'll make it this time, but you've got to get your shit together.' Well, I broke down and cried my eyes out while he held me. He was solid! My nose was running, and he reached into the inside breast pocket of his favorite black suit, God Emma, it was the one he was buried in! He handed me a handkerchief to blow my nose. I looked at him, but before I could speak, he sort of drifted away like a cloud of smoke. His visit changed my life, that's why I joined."

Donna's eyes were filled with tears. Emma reached into her purse for a crumpled Kleenex and handed it to Donna.

Donna wiped her eyes, then balled the Kleenex in her hand. She dug into her purse.

"Here, look. This is his handkerchief."

Spasms of goose bumps raced up and down Emma's back and arms, especially when her eyes riveted on the large, off-white linen handkerchief with the embroidered initials of Donna's father.

"Can you see why I'm here?"

Emma said nothing while she continued shivering.

They were joined by both men. Jack was carrying a large tray holding a brown porcelain tea pot and four brown mugs. Emma selected a mint herbal tea bag from the tray and bobbed it several times in her mug while she thought about what Donna had told her.

"I thought I would go into some basics before the others joined us for the séance." Karl Michael scrutinized the two women while he poured hot water into his mug.

"Your bracelet...sort of shook me up last night. Did Donna tell you what happened?"

Emma nodded yes.

"I didn't detail everything to the study circle last night. It scared the hell out of me! I've never had anything like that happen to me before. The vibrations from the bracelet were incredible--I almost felt like his force was in me, a really weird sensation!"

Karl stared into his mug for a few moments of contemplation while he mentally rehashed what had happened. He quietly sipped from the mug then sat it down on a water-spotted, marble-topped side table next to his chair.

"It was him, Rudolph Valentino. I not only saw him, I heard him. I honestly can't remember too much of what transpired because it lasted for only a few seconds I think, could have been a minute, anyway, he did say something rather cryptic."

Karl drilled Emma with his intense cobalt-blue eyes: "He said that I 'will' get you here, Emma, for a séance tonight."

Emma continued to grow more uncomfortable, not only from his penetrating stare but also with his statement. Valentino meant nothing to her, but still, it reawakened something in her that she couldn't quite firmly grasp, something at the back of her mind that lurked, waiting for discovery.

Karl broke into her thoughts. "Before the others join us, I will sketch a brief outline of where we are headed tonight." He paused while he took another sip of tea, continuing, "The word séance is French for sitting. The people that assemble for a séance are called sitters, and the person that conducts the séance is called a medium or a sensitive. The actual séance has been with mankind since early civilization in one form or another. When it takes on a religious overtone, such as when Christianity becomes mixed in this multi-flavored pudding, it's called Spiritualism. Séances are not meant for the worshiping of the dead or necromancy, it is merely an attempt to contact the dead, our dearly departed. True Spiritualists believe that when we die, we move on to another life. Some divide this new world, or new spirit life, into astral planes. I've heard from others that there are as many as eight to fourteen different planes, or levels, with our particular planet being close to the first plane. Others have said that the spirit world runs parallel to ours, but the vibrational energy is so different from ours that we seldom can see or hear them--spirits, that is. Occasionally there are cracks in this "cosmic egg" which trap some of them in our lower vibrational field."

He paused for another sip of tea and to catch his breath. Emma knew from his trembling voice tone that he was excited about these subjects and could spend hours in speaking and debate.

Karl cleared his throat, and immediately went into what he had been talking about before his interruption.

"We call them ghosts or spirit entities. Sometimes a person, such as me, can be clairvoyant, clairaudient, clairsentient, or sometimes all three, which means that we can see, hear and sense these spirit entities. I know for sure that I can receive messages from trapped spirits on our earth plane. And, I don't feel that it is sick or morbid to contact those souls that have left us, it's simply a natural progression of things that we were meant to do. Emma, I've devoted my life to the metaphysical sciences, wanting desperately to make this an accepted science from which all of mankind could benefit. Just think, if people knew that life continues in a different form, and that a person who leads a life of dishonor while alive, and inflicts it on others...then there could be dreadful paybacks. It would also remove the anguish of finality from our lives. Wow, sorry to be so long winded and boorish. There is so much more I could say, right, Donna?"

Emma, now very much interested, spoke, "Where did you get these unusual abilities from, did they just happen?"

"When I was eleven I was hit by a car while

riding a bicycle. I was in a coma for over two weeks, and then I suddenly snapped out of it. The powers were with me, as a matter of fact. I went from a solid D student to an A student without any trouble, became a pretty decent athlete—hockey and lacrosse, and later sailed through three degrees in college. The substantial sums of money I made in land development aided by these special gifts, helped pay for this building, two bad marriages, and along with very generous gifts like Donnas', have assisted in building our respectability. But I always felt like a freak, a genuine outcast from society. Can you imagine what it would be like to hear people's thoughts and see their futures? At times I thought I was crazed. Then it came to me in a dream--what I was meant for."

Emma asked, "So you mean that you picked up these abilities when you almost died?"

"Yes. It's not at all uncommon. Many people I've talked with over the years...well, it seems that certain life threatening events, like severe illnesses, Near Death and Out of Body Experiences, bring on these wonderful psychic gifts."

Donna broke in and stood up. "I think I'll go outside and have a cigarette before we start. Em, want one?"

"No, perhaps afterwards."

Six people sat around a well polished mahogany table in the 'receiving' room. Three walls held floor to ceiling book shelves filled with multi-colored leather bound books, none of the titles or authors recognizable to Emma. The other wall held the door and two small oil paintings of a forest scene and a Rocky Mountain sunset.

The windowless room was large and vault quiet, the only sound, Emma was sure, was her heart wildly thumping in her chest cavity. She was scared, not over what was going to happen, but over what she might find out. The hair at the back of her neck seemed to be loaded with electricity. Her finger tips tingled with anticipation.

She looked around the table at the sitters whom she had just met. Donna's eyes were open wide and alert. Jack Sewell was swallowing hard. Karl was pale and relaxed. Estelle Mendoza plucked at the lint on her black dress. The face of a handsome Denver police detective, Robert Shell, was void of any expression, smiling only when he caught Emma's eyes. Since he was sitting directly across from her she had shyly dropped her eyes and feigned staring at the mirror-like finish of the table. She blushed several times when their eyes had met.

"Well, I would like to mention again that our guest, Emma Glass, whom we met during a few seconds of introductions, is a novice to all of this, so as we progress during this sitting I will explain a few things for her benefit."

Emma looked at Donna, who winked encouragement.

"When we activate our spirit quest by touching each others' hands, thereby commencing a bond of energy and protection, nobody must leave this circle of protection! Sometimes these sittings are a hit-and-miss affair...but I hope that you will keep a clear and open mind to ensure Mr. Rudolph Valentino's entry into our world. Emma has an item of Valentino's that I used with another study group last night--loaded with his vibrations, I believe; I feel I should make another attempt at contact again. This time we will see if we can talk to Mr. Valentino. Again—please, no talking and do not leave the protection of this circle."

Jack stood and lowered the dimmer switch on the door wall behind him. After he sat down, Karl commenced deep breathing when he closed his eyes. All of the participants joined hands when Karl closed his eyes, creating a power focus of energy and protection.

The room was completely still, the only sounds coming from the sitter's soft breathing in unison, which Emma soon joined.

Ten minutes into deep breathing, almost on cue, the sitters broke their grasp with their neighbor's hands and placed their hands, palms down on the table, spreading their hands, which allowed them to touch their neighbor's small fingers. Through all of these movements their eyes were closed in meditation and deep breathing.

"I call upon the White Light for protection and love."

Emma opened her eyes slightly to watch Karl's invocation.

"I bring the Eternal Forces into our bodies, asking for the White Light's protection and guidance." Karl slowly repeated this invocation three times in a mesmerizing voice.

Emma squinted her eyes while scanning the room, jolting at what she saw. Karl seemed to be completely surrounded in a transparent, shimmering, foggy white light. The light clung tightly to his body while pulsating like a soft, glowing neon light tube whose gases are first dim, then bright, and then dim again.

His eyes were wide open, riveted straight ahead at nothing she could discern. He was in trance.

"We are here to establish contact with Rudolph Valentino. Emma Glass is also here. I ask for the protection and guidance of my spirit guide, Rosemary McLean. May I please speak with her?"

It was silent for a few seconds. Karl then spoke aloud, "Yes, I'm ready. Yes…I'm not sure…I was told--Yes, she's here. I don't understand, would you say that again? Why?"

Emma shivered as a cold draft of air suddenly surrounded her. She cleared her throat and prepared herself for what, she wasn't sure of. She opened her eyes slowly, noting that Karl was staring ahead eyes wide and unblinking, and that the other sitter's eyes were still closed.

Donna looked like she was sleeping. Karl's milky transparent aura continued to softly pulsate, it either emanated from his body or it was hung over him. Emma mentally struggled with logic and belief, then suspended her logic, realizing it didn't really matter-- this séance was really happening!

Suddenly, from out of the corner of her right eye she saw movement. Several black fuzzy spots, almost circular in shape, not more than two feet in diameter, floated across the room then drifted slowly above Karl's head, and just as quickly moved to the ceiling where they seemed to cling. She shuddered again, almost violently, knowing that evil had entered the room--or death....

Both had. If the sitters had seen and understood these malevolent spirit entities they would have died from fright and disgust. Luckily for Emma, they didn't know she had observed their presence.

Six evil, departed demon-souls drifted above the séance participants, none having the best of intentions. They snarled and moaned about their discomfort over being attracted to the light and the voice that had awakened them. They looked down on the man who was communicating through their open door, and almost on signal swirled around his vulnerable life force.

A blinding, violet-colored light burst through the invisible gateway, brilliant and flickering with such intensity that the entities regrouped on the ceiling and their turn at fear. The light was a force far greater than their feeble strength could ever muster. With the realization the violet-colored light was a much higher developed spirit entity, they hung suspended in the north corner shadows of the room while they waited for the powerful spirit guide to come through the portal; they would then escape back through the same doorway to the safety of other side.

Karl's head dropped forward, broad chin digging into his upper sternum; he moaned while his body was racked with spasms, stopping only when the disembodied presence entered the room.

"Thank you for inviting me to your little gathering. It has been so long! My Earth Plane, my birth place! I have much to say, but I promise that I will not overstay my welcome and unduly upset your leader, at least for tonight."

Emma's eyes searched the shadows of the room, wondering where the soft-accented voice had come from. She felt the sensation of cob webs lightly brushing against her face. She looked up to meet the coal-black eyes of Valentino.

Valentino's murky apparition floated several feet above the middle of the table, naked and one dimensional, at times seeming to scrape against the high ceiling of the room. His spirit was a gauzy, faded, out of focus blur except for his handsome face.

He spoke to Emma in a soft, conspiratorial voice, almost like he was intending to seduce her: "Are you the one with my slave bracelet, my gift of love?"

Emma knew she looked like a drooling idiot with an open mouth and a forgotten voice.

"You have nothing to fear, granddaughter of Reba Walizuski, eh, Tonopolski." Emma chilled at the mention of her maternal grandmother's name. She grew frightened because he knew about her!

"I gave dear Reba the love bracelet after I passed over. I left her with a damning curse too, first in spite, later tempering this anger when I learned the wisdom that comes from death. Why should I remain forever angry?"

Valentino quickly changed from a transparent specter into a solid materialization. He was darkly handsome and athletic in build. He seemed to be 'real'. Too real...Emma felt close to fainting! Her heart pumped faster with increased panic. Her temples throbbed. Sweat appeared on her forehead despite the coolness of the room. She was entering the stages of shock.

"Please forgive my lack of modesty, we seldom wear our robes."

She felt a cold draft whip by her head and she looked up. Valentino was wrapped in a body length, silver-hued robe, the hood resting on his broad shoulders. He was still floating above the table and his handsome face was less than two feet from hers. Emma noticed that even though he was seemingly suspended above the séance table, his robe did not flutter open.

"Better?" He smiled, revealing a mouth of even, small white teeth. "It is like having a first rendezvous, you don't want to show everything all at once." He laughed at his weak joke.

With a sudden fluid motion he spun around the table while coasting above it, stopping to peer into each tranced face around the table, darting to each sitter like a humming bird in a quest for the sweetest flower. In seconds he had completed an inventory of each participant. He spun back to face a disbelieving Emma.

"Fascinating. A high-minded group. It is rather unusual to see six people at one time with a thirst for the eternal knowledge of truth, especially you, cara mia. However, seeing their sins and knowing their future is not a good thing."

He paused from talking and quickly looked around at the participants. Valentino stared intensely for several moments at Emma, his brooding eyes piercing and somehow knowing. She felt his thoughts probing her mind.

"Can you really handle the truth? No, I don't think so, not yet, because you are going to travel an unusual road soon, filled with revelations to sort out on your own. I'm very sorry that you have suffered such pain over your husband's death, but

I can also assure you that Travis is quite happy in Summerland...or so I've been told. Lost love is indeed a terrible thing cara mia. I cannot go to where your Travis is until I'm finished with a certain special Earth Plane matter; you will fully understand this problem of mine--which does involve you, when it is time to be revealed."

Valentino did a quick spin and looked at Robert Shell, saying, "So, this is the one...interesting! He will bear watching by you." He looked directly again at Emma while he smiled.

With the mention of Travis's name, Emma's eyes had pooled with tears. Valentino tenderly wiped her eyes with cool hands. She shuddered from the cold, yet sensual contact. She felt very strange and somehow out of control. He captured her hands, drawing them to his mouth while smothering her palms with his chilled lips. She shivered again, this time from the sexual vibrations of his kisses.

"Ah, love, nothing will ever take its place! I wonder if my fans and my lovers actually ever shed such honest tears of grief for me. Any way, I still miss them—especially my lovers."

Emma remained captivated by his intense liquid brown eyes, and knowing exactly why so many women had loved him. Breathless with a fleeting surge of desire, she was embarrassed and unnerved. She hastily looked around the table to break her thoughts.

"They can't see or hear me. Only your leader knows what is happening even though he appears to be unconscious."

Valentino became grave. "I want my love bracelet back. When we do apports from my side—an apport is when we materialize objects to your side, things such as that bracelet came from my side. They can be thrown over to your side, but it is almost impossible for you to pass them over here. My dear Emma, I don't mean to make jest of the pain that damnable bracelet has brought your family, but I must tell you to be on guard at all times and take seriously the matters of the spirit world. Stay alert! It might save you. Please attend these meetings--ah, séances as often as you are instructed--through your dreams or by way of a medium. I have asked you not to speak because I do not want your voice known over here. Will you come back to the next sitting? Nod your head yes, it's for your own safety. I don't think it's too late. Everything is in motion now."

Emma looked at his pale spirit face, seeing that he was being very frank, and nodded in the affirmative.

"Very good, I look forward to seeing you again, soon!"

He disappeared. She looked around the table at the other sitters, then at Karl's exhausted face. She remained still for several minutes, digesting what had happened while waiting for her tablemates to exit their trance.

Looking at Emma, Karl spoke after leaving trance, "How about that—incredible! I am so privileged to see this."

She managed to project false confidence, which she did not have--at all, and said, "Yes." She had had the hell scared out of her. Valentino left her with two questions unanswered. What did he mean about the pain the bracelet had brought her family, and what things were in motion?

In low voice, Karl said, "This visitation is what happens when a particular spirit or guide wishes or demands communication. Do you remember what I told you about how spirit communication can be a one-on-one affair? What happened tonight is a perfect example, I honestly believe. Emma you had communication with a spirit entity this night, the Rudolph Valentino. Although we all heard and saw what transpired, it was erased from our minds for our personal protection, perhaps sanity."

Karl stared down Emma for emphasis, obviously concerned and very much disturbed, knowing full well that "it" was now beginning.

"I think we'd better call it a night. Estelle, would you please call down the White Light of Protection for our safe journey home?" They clasped each other's hands while standing in an energy circle of love and protection. When Estelle completed the invocation, Karl said, "Till we meet again, and may the protection of our guardian spirits be with each of us."

Karl forced a smile. "Emma and Donna, I would like to speak with both of you for just a few minutes, if I may."

While Karl and Jack saw the others out and locked up, Donna plopped down on the couch, emotionally drained.

"Whew, see what I mean? I don't know about you, but I feel like I've been slammed, and I don't really know why." Donna was visibly shaken. For once she wasn't a drama queen.

Emma sat next to Donna on the couch, her head spinning. "I had no idea that séances were for real. It goes against everything I've ever learned. My scientific logic has just been thrown out the door! And now I realize that it is not a hoax."

"Believe dear, very strongly, in what happened tonight. No mirrors or mumbo-jumbo. I know what I felt like when it first happened to me. It scared the living crap out of me!"

Emma mulled over her thoughts, finally shooting out, "You know this means there is life after death. Donna, I only wish you could have seen him!"

"Honey, forget everything you once believed about death. I never told you about my uncle the Rabbi, God, he even nags me from over there; then my older brother, Benjamin, well, that's another story. One thing for sure...you'll never be the same again!"

Before Emma could ask Donna any questions, Karl and Jack returned to the room.

They moved their chairs closer to the women sitting on the couch. Jack's face was totally blank. Karl searched Emma's thoughts, and read only confusion and panic, then reached into the pocket of his very English tweed sports coat.

"Here, I'd better give this back."

He handed her the gold slave bracelet wrapped in a small bubble wrapped bag.

"The vibrations from the bracelet aren't quite so shocking when they're wrapped up. I heard what he said. Damn, I even saw him. Amazing! This was a real shocker! I wish I could have had this sitting on video. Could you think of what this would do to our smug society? Valentino's soul force was purposeful and strong, revealing his unique personality that has refused to fade away in death. "

Emma muttered, "He said that I was the only one who could hear or see him."

"Well, not really. I guess he didn't realize—if he really did care, that my clairaudient and clairvoyant powers are pretty acute, but I do know he gave you a warning. I need time to think about the visit and the significance of the bracelet, and its tie in with your historical family. Everything about this session was unusual. A very strange request for your attendance--and that warning. This is a rare occurrence."

When Karl looked at Jack for confirmation, Jack was in deep thought while his hands nervously stroked his knees. Jack had a dead-pan look etched across his face and when he realized they were looking at him, he nodded his head like he had been listening.

Then he spoke, "Did anyone feel, or notice that .something else was in the room? I really felt that something disturbing was in the room, you know Karl, like when we were doing that series of séances in Vancouver."

He received no acknowledgment to his statement.

Emma remained quiet, not knowing what to say about the dark shadows on the wall and the ceiling. She dropped the gold bracelet into her purse and stood up. "I'm exhausted, It's time for me to go, oh, yes it is! This evening has been far more than I had bargained for." She smiled at her understatement.

Karl said, "If you need me--anytime, I want you to call me, do you understand, Emma, anytime. I hope you won't shrug this off. I'll be in contact with you when the next sitting is arranged." He thrust a business card at her, which she put into her purse without reading.

She sped down a tree lined, darkly shrouded, Evans Avenue at break-neck speed to get to her house in Chamberlain Park, sure that the Furies were after her. When she arrived she delayed entry to the empty house, sitting in the car for twenty minutes while staring at the white, three story, Queen Anne Revival house built in 1910. Travis had lovingly restored the derelict mansion brick by brick, board by board over a period of six years. The sixteen room house had been purchased for entertaining and the children that never came.

The half moon blinked through puffy tufts of clouds, tracing spider-webbed patterns through leaves and branches, twisting and distorting the shadows across the high gables of the roof. The bone-white painted house took on the look of a phony Hollywood backstage set; Emma felt that the eerie look of the house complemented this very strange evening.

A very strange night. Her empirical research in anthropology had not prepared her for the paranormal. She felt the studies of ancient and present day peoples somehow were seasoned and mixed with a sauce of unreliable supernatural events, mainly ignored by the skeptical twenty-first century mind. Now, she was confronted with a new insight.

As a professor, her lectures and papers for journals had always been scholastically researched and presented with footnotes and data, precisely referencing any reliable source and explanation. Dry and logical, concrete and scholarly, leaving no room for speculation, and certainly allowing no latitude for esoterical speculation and the paranormal. She had long ago formulated rigid standards in her research; She knew she would be considered a prime grade A kook if she had ever used the material of this night.

Emma sighed as she made her way to the front door. She sighed again when the key opened the door. She was alone again.

Chapter 3

She dropped her purse and keys onto the hall table after turning on the lights. Gliding through the long front living room, which had once been a receiving parlor for visitors, the reek of a strong scent, sweet and cloying, hung in the air, a flower based perfume, sexual in its brashness. It was not the cleaning woman's cologne, her cleaning day was Wednesday, and Emma remembered that she had thrown out the last of the flowers, four dozen roses that Tom had wired from Portland, besides, her cleaning lady never smelled that good. She turned on the kitchen lights and walked to the refrigerator. Looking into the massive, stainless steel commercial refrigerator she identified nothing that interested her, deciding a cup of herbal tea and sea toast slathered with raspberry jam would take the edge off of her nervousness.

Making her way up the stairs to the master bedroom, carefully balancing the plate of sea toast in one hand and the mug of tea in the other, she was still feeling strange. The struggling moonlight brought enough light into the bedroom for her to set the plate and mug down on a small, marble topped cigarette table next to the fireplace. The room was close and reeked of the heady flower-based perfume.

Emma flipped on the light switch which immediately lit three bedroom lamps. She opened two of the French doors near the bed then turned on the stereo system, loading a CD of Vivaldi's 'Four Seasons'. The room was flooded with the first movement.

She dug through the second drawer of the vanity table and found a half-filled bottle of prescription Valium. She shook out two pink tablets and sat down in the winged back chair, washing the pills down with tea, then propped her feet on the ottoman while she waited for the tingle of paralysis to deaden her nerve endings.

After becoming woozy she floated to the king-sized, four poster bed. She shed her clothes, dropping them at the foot of the bed; sandwiching herself in the embrace of the Wedgewood blue colored satin sheets, the Vivaldi CD mellowed her keyed up mood while she stretched and yawned, falling quickly into the tight embrace of sleep.

The dream induced by Valium arrived quickly.

VALENTINO'S CURSE

Valentino stood next to the bed. He crawled into bed, pulling the bedclothes over his ethereal body. At first he nuzzled her neck with his cool lips, then his hands explored her body, gently at first, then faster, sweeping over her unresisting body. Emma moaned in pleasure when he softly squeezed her erect nipples in his cool, but not cold hands, moaning louder when his fingers prepared his entry.

On her back now, her hands squeezed his muscular back and buttock muscles. She moaned at his entry. She savored the realism of the dream enough to smell his sweet cold breath in her face and the flickering tongue that entered her mouth.

Emma slipped further into deep sleep, awakening only when the telephone rang. She stretched in pleasure and allowed the answering machine to capture the call on the fourth ring.

Slowly scanning the bedroom, she watched sunlight paint the room through ivory colored sheers. The sounds of a cranky lawn mower cutting grass in the nearby park brought her back to reality.

Blushing from the faint memory of the erotic dream and a gut-wrenching orgasm, her eyes focused fleetingly on the ceiling, then swept through the bed room. She rolled on the cool satin sheets, sitting up in terror!

A red rose lay on the pillow next to her, its petals almost completely open. Emma stared at the object in fright. It could have been a coiled snake because of the horror she felt.

A guttural, animal sound escaped from somewhere deep in her throat, leaving her quivering mouth in a shriek.

"Damn, damn, damn!" She knew it was not possible. Another audible scream left her mouth. "God damn it, this is not happening!"

She sprung from the bed, trying to flee the rose that now seemed close to striking her. She flew to the dressing closet, pulling, almost tearing, a navy blue robe from the hanger which she struggled to belt tightly on her shuddering body.

Emma crept back into the bedroom. The rose still lay on the pillow, its red color glowing brighter with her vanishing control. Thoughts of the séance and spirit sex were too much to deal with. She collapsed on the floor.

Hot prickles of gushing water from three shower heads temporarily negated the imagined violation. Several times she scrubbed her body hard with a Loofa sponge while mentally attempting to reason herself through the nightmare. If it had been a dream--of course it had been a dream, then where did the rose come from? Any woman knew when she had been violated, but by a ghost, a thing? Impossible! Fuzzy Valium thoughts! Emma was off balance. And then fearfully expectant: would it happen again? She blushed, making up her mind that she would never, ever, use Valium again.

Chapter 4

The library was comforting. A stable, safe and known environment. It had been a long time since she had escaped into the stacks of the Penrose Library. Her laptop had provided some of her research information. The Internet had taken away a lot of the pleasure in visiting a library. E books and downloads also did not cut it with her. Hell, she used her iPod a few times than "lost" it somewhere in the library. She pitied the student that had to listen to her downloads of classical music mixed with the Rolling Stones, but she thought, like our lives, everything can and is eventually deleted.

Welcome smells of book paper and printing ink, mixed with that certain essence of library dust, put her at ease. The familiar. The reliable. The Internet could never come close to the pleasures of paging through books at a leisure pace.

Emma dearly loved the bells-and-whistles cell phone Tom had insisted that she have, and her wide screen lap top—which assisted her mightily in writing her present book and research papers, had all been wonderful gadgets, but she still felt the comfort of a snail pace of pen on paper that assisted her more in the assembling and organization of thoughts. Travis had classified these periods of Emma's reverie as her time of 'Simplicity of Spiritual Enlightenment'.

She spent the better part of the day searching through a book-locating computer, later happily searching for miss-shelved books which added to the thrill of the hunt and diverting her mind from unpleasant thoughts.

Emma skimmed through volume after volume on the paranormal and related subjects which kept her busy jotting and scribbling in two fat spiral notebooks. The volumes on so-called primitive spirit worship, ESP, Voodoo and Zombies: 'Faces In The Smoke' by Gersi, and 'Instant ESP' by David St. Clair were particularly exciting finds; these were followed by the 'Time-Life' series on the paranormal and twelve other subject-related books.

Noises from students, and in particular a couple making out in the stacks distracted her at first, but when she thumbed through the catch of books, she found interesting information on the spirit world, and the young lover's distractions faded. Fragmented pictures of the séance and her ghost lovemaking came into focus. She realized that she was not an exceptional victim.

She ran across numerous cases, true or imagined, of similar violations, but she dismissed her personal experience as Valium induced. Also the thought: just because it was in print did not make it so, that these incidents actually happened. This attempt at pure logic was quickly pushed away. Emma knew something bizarre had happened, and only Karl Michael and Jack Sewell could assist her in arriving at some sort of reasonable explanation. She had to find out why it had happened...and if it was going to happen again.

When she was ready to leave the library, she knew she would have to look for one last book. The search for Valentino was easy. She hurriedly poured over a hefty coffee table sized book on past silent movie Hollywood stars.

Rudolph Valentino was a first magnitude star of early Hollywood in the nineteen twenties. A poor Italian immigrant, he quickly rose to stardom because of his dancing ability and an inordinate amount of charisma which splashed onto the silent screen. He had several successful films, the best received being "The Sheik" and "The Son of the Sheik." Married twice, His most notable wife was

VALENTINO'S CURSE

Natacha Rambova. He died from a mysterious complication, the autopsy concluded, from Peritonitis. He was Thirty-one years of age, dying an early death on August 23, 1926.

He had a famous condom named after him, several poems, and was recorded singing on a record which was a hit.

Emma deduced his screen life had been short but exciting. His death was a carnival of the catastrophic, riots by thousands of fans across the world, mainly by women. Even suicides. A short, vibrant life annotated with several black and white silent movies.

She thrilled in spite of herself; had she really met him, had spiritual sex, perhaps, but how could she logically explain away the rose, and did she really have one of his slave bracelets, which according to family lore she did have, but, the séance at the church should had proven to her that she had indeed met him. Did she really meet him at the séance? She had been in an emotional state for some time, ever since Travis's death, and as far as the sexual dream, well, perhaps it could be explained away as her therapist had said: "Dreams take the fear we give them—they are birthed and live through our encouragement."

The Bull and Crown Pub on north Cherry Creek Drive groaned with an overflow dinner crowd. Emma took the last available table in a dark corner next to the bar. She went over her notes, occasionally taking a deep sip of wine when she found some particularly interesting facts. Spiritualism had struck a resonate chord with her for some odd reason. She caught herself thinking along this line. For some odd reason? What a joke! It wasn't odd, it could be considered a real nightmare.

The séance had not relied on Tarot cards, Ouija board, table tipping, and certainly no trumpets were blown by specters or tambourines struck by ghostly hands. The séance appeared to be above board, and the sitters certainly did not seem to be in need of psychiatric assistance. As a matter of fact, the handsome Denver police detective was a possible indication of the legitimacy of the sitting.

Donna Epstein was a little flaky at times, but her Jewish show me attitude was used full measure before she would jump into something that smacked of being kooky.

The waitress came by the table for the third time asking for her order, and after being curtly dismissed, slinked away from Emma's table and waited on three well-dressed young men sitting next to her table.

She looked up again, noticing a much too young blond man staring at her. Her eyes quickly darted to the front door wishing Donna would walk into the Pub.

Emma's ego glowed from a young man's attempt at picking her up, but she was also annoyed with the thought of being targeted as an easy pick up. Was she painted with a large availability sign? She remembered the classes she had taught at the university and the presumptuous young male students--grade hunting or real interest? She also remembered Donna's motto: "If it has tires or testicles, then expect trouble."

The bar turned into a meat market, crammed with the evening shift of serious drinking professionals some eager for one night stands. Emma looked at her watch in agitation, six-thirty and no Donna. She flipped through the two-inch high stack of spiral notebooks for a third time; ten more minutes, then she was gone.

Quickly scanning the bar filled with young faces and hard bodies, she convinced herself that her feet were now firmly planted on the treadmill of middle age...and oblivion. If it hadn't been for Travis's brother Tom, she knew she was going to live the rest of her life as an old widow professing easy credit courses at the university.

She still suffered periodic episodes of an anxiety reaction-formation, linked, according to her therapist, to Travis and her parent's deaths. She still couldn't shake her parents deaths even though it was years ago. Travis's extinction seemed a few hours ago.

Faint memories of her loving mother and father and abusive foster homes, were again able to take renewed life lately. The old poisons of loneliness and self-pity mixed in a concoction of despair, and in the sensation of being off balance. She loathed these feelings, tired of her self-pity.

Now she was faced with the possibility of life after death. Proof? She saw Valentino--she thought, he talked to her...she even had sex with him--perhaps. She had to believe again in something. What would happen if it was all true and she could meet Travis on the other side? What would she say about Tom? Would Travis understand that she needed someone that knew her and cared for her? She did care for Tom very much.

Sex with a spook. Sex with Tom. Guilt took the form of a winged beast with shadows fluttering across her thoughts, perching on the core of her real guilt, the year long affair with Travis's younger brother. She could feel the talons of depression dig deeper into her free-floating anxiety, but she knew that she was tired of repressing her emotions, she had to break loose.

Her extensive academic studies in anthropology had shown her that the most primitive of societies, including many modern cultures, believed in some sort of continuance after death. What was there to doubt now?

She noticed she had heavily underlined a quote from the French philosopher, Jean-Jacques Rosseau: "I have too much suffered in this life not to expect another one. All the subtleties of metaphysics will not make me doubt for a minute the immortality of the soul and a beneficent Providence. I know it, I believe it, I wish it, I hope it, and I will uphold it to my last breath."

It was not clear why the quote was so profound to her at the moment she had written it down, but it fit her foot like a sock.

She made an asterisk to research other philosophers on this subject. Metaphysics had always been viewed by her as philosophical clap trap, now she felt there might be some grains of truth for her to sift through.

Then the matter of the séance, which had shattered a basic belief she once had held, that once your dead, you're still dead. Emma felt she had painted herself in a corner.

Several of the books she had skimmed through in the university library had been written by the American and English Societies for Psychical Research, the quintessential heart of the 1890's renewed Spiritualist movement, which held thousands of seemingly well-researched, first and second-hand case studies of ghosts, hauntings and life after death essays. Granted they were not committed under modern scientific laboratory standards, with optimum control conditions set up by research scientists.

"Well, it looks like I'm late again. Forgive me?"

Emma looked up into the harried eyes of Donna.

"Damn garage, you'd think they would have parts for a BMW--in a BMW garage, no less!"

"Don't apologize, I was rather hoping you'd be late. I was almost picked up by a young blond man behind you. Don't look!" She giggled.

"I need booze, something in my veins besides tired blood. Goddamn, what a shit day, pardon my French!"

They both ordered drinks, Donna a Vodka Martini, and Emma a wine spritzer. The waitress dropped her snotty smile when she saw the killing look in Donna's eyes.

The conversation held to small talk while they ate small portions of an overdone London Broil and a soggy garden house salad. When they had finished, Donna leaned back, gulping down her second drink.

"Well, why are we meeting?"

Emma repressed her annoyance.

"Why do you think? I wanted to talk about what happened in the séance."

"Why? I have a fairly good idea of what occurred. It should be a private thing for you, at least for a while. You know, Em, there's more yet to come. Don't you?" Donna's eyes were wide open and unblinking.

Emma was momentarily confused. "I don't understand."

"What I meant was, well...the door has been opened for you. Believe me, when I say nothing just happens by chance. You've been contacted, whether you like it or not, to receive messages from the other side. It might be Travis acting through a stronger control, like Valentino. I honestly believe that Travis or somebody who was once close to you, is trying to get your attention. The bracelet was the magnet to get you to the séance."

Emma interrupted. "God, this is the weirdest thing I've ever been through. I'd love to tell you what happened to me during the sitting, and what happened last night, but I'm scared. This stuff isn't real, well it's real I guess, but I'm a little frightened and damned confused."

Donna drained her glass, almost gagging when the Vodka seared her throat. "How do you think I felt when my dad appeared...and all of the other things that happened before I went to see Karl Michael. Trust me, you know me better than that, I don't seek out these things."

Donna stared at her half emptied salad plate, thinking about how she twice had been saved from suicide by intervening spirits. She came close to revealing what had happened, then decided to remain silent.

"I want to know what happened, please." Emma's voice was almost shrill in its demand.

Donna flushed a bright pink, close to telling, then thought better of it. "No, not yet. It's much too private at this point. But I'll say this, it was very, very real and something else...it's changed me forever, giving me a different perspective on my life."

They looked at each other for several minutes, not speaking, both faces inscrutable. Young voices grew in liquored volume, along with the clink of crockery and glasses; not enough distraction to derail their mind chatter though. They were in a silent draw, an oasis of quiet in the bedlam surrounding them.

Finally Emma broke the silence. "I spent the better part of the day at the university library, doing research on the paranormal. I ran across numerous references on Spiritualism, particularly on the séance. I had no problems with what I read, I just had no idea that so much had been written on the subject. Well, I know what happened during this séance. To be frank, I have a fairly good handle on what this one was all about."

Donna replied, "Oh, Really? In the three months that I've been taking spiritual unfoldment classes with Karl Michael, I found out a lot. I struggled with my Jewish conscious to out guess the old Hebrew tribal concerns with demons, spirits, guilt, et. cetera, but my experiences were, correction, are, the best things that have happened to me. You know of course, that women are considered the best candidates for mediumship."

Donna moved closer to Emma, then patted Emma's right hand which was nervously stroking an empty wine glass.

"Brass tacks time, Em. Look, I carry something in my purse, let me read it to you. It's a Jewish guilt trip, especially when I feel I've gone too far...and when I experience too much hubris it brings me down to earth."

Donna dug deeply into a flashy Gucci purse in which she dug out a ratty looking piece of folded paper. She unfolded the square, smoothing the fold lines on the table: "His breath goeth forth, he returneth to his earth; on that very day his thoughts perish; Psalms l46:4'."

Donna paused, then continued quoting from the paper while not once looking at the paper: "The living know that they shall die; but the dead know not anything. Their love, and their hatred, and their envy, is now perished; neither have they any more a portion forever in anything that is done under the sun. There is no work, nor device, nor knowledge, nor wisdom, in the grave, whither thou goest, Ecclesiastes 9:5."

Donna's eyes almost burned holes in the paper. She held her thoughts for a moment while she refolded the paper and stuffed it slowly into her purse, pausing to control her emotions.

"I carry this as a reminder to examine every thing closely. You, of all people, know that I'm not the most religious person that every walked--hell, not even close. But I carry these quotes to stabilize and temper myself from leaping completely into something that

I'm not experienced in. I know, without a shadow of a doubt, that there's life after death--we've both brushed shoulders with the so called 'grand and final answers'. Honey, I don't want to talk about this anymore--at least for a while, do you mind? Let's guess which young hunk would roll the best in the hay."

Emma immediately agreed, surprised at how easily Donna surrendered a one way discussion. Highly unusual. She also noticed how tightly clenched her friend's jaw was. Emma felt light headed from three double wine spritzes and "tainted" with thoughts of a single red rose on her pillow and the enjoyed spirit sex it represented.

Emma could feel the growing pressure of a migraine. She had forgotten her medication and knew the rolling thunderstorm in her head was drawing closer. She had about thirty minutes until the storm broke loose.

"I've got to go. One of my killer migraines is coming, and I left the pills at home. Thanks for listening. Call me tomorrow." Emma dug into her purse, finding three twenty dollar bills which she dropped on the table, air kissed Donna on the cheek, and quickly waded through the riptide of bodies to the parking lot.

Chapter 5

Emma cursed out loud as she sped out of the medical building's parking lot. She was furious about the one hour visit with Dr. Kohen, which again resulted in her pouring her guts out, and his doing nothing to stop the self-mutilation; he listened patiently, occasionally wagging his head in neutral sympathy. His inscrutable face observed Emma while his nubby, liver-spotted hands rapidly jotted cryptic notes onto a steno pad.

She had been seeing the therapist for almost two years, sometimes twice a week, for $360 an hour. For the past five months it had been a one hour session every other two weeks--with anti-depressants on an as needed basis.

Dr. Kohen had unlocked and partially released the pain that had driven much of her life, helping to somewhat temper the anger and guilt she had over Travis's death--leaving her to drown in a mainly inconsequential existence and she remained furious with Kohen for not giving her the total relief she demanded.

She desperately wanted to tell him about the séance and Valentino. Emma hid that happening behind another door, hoping that Kohen would see the bread crumb trail of her hints, but all he wanted was verbiage on Travis and Tom.

Dr. Marvin Kohen had been mildly taken back at the mental deterioration of Emma when she had first commenced sessions by herself. There had been two with Travis in attendance. Now, he had been worried enough for her emotional being to schedule blocks of two hour appointments, twice a week, for the first year of her individual therapy. After those sessions, he felt confident she was able to control her suicidal tendencies--with the assistance of medication, prescription of course, and Tom's love.

The single most important outcome she had gleaned from the never ending therapy sessions had been Dr. Kohen's idea of Emma's personal journal. At first she viewed these journals as merely being a girl's diary blurbs, but later found much solace and comfort in writing down eventful happenings and personal thoughts.

She now had eleven leather bound volumes which she kept hidden in the bedroom safe; not even Tom was aware of these journals. Periodically she would review what she had written, and actually could see the progress she had made. Just by reading these jottings she began to understand her moods, and the growing disassociation from a very troubled past.

She continued to curse her psychiatrist through the heavy Evans Avenue traffic and at every red light. Medication was not the answer. Emma knew she had garnered a new shield of protection through therapy and additional strength through the physical and emotional love she had received from Tom. Her survival was no longer in question.

Tom's late model yellow Corvette was parked in the driveway and despite her ragged anger, was relieved to have him back in the house.

The mail was neatly stacked on the hall credenza, which she quickly sorted through, the bulk hitting the small brass trash can to the side of the credenza. Tom's black leather flight bags were sitting in the hallway, and she was mildly surprised that Tom had not taken the bags up to the bedroom, he really must be tired, she thought. It was unlike him. Ever since she had known him, he had had a neurotic disposition for tidiness and order.

VALENTINO'S CURSE

She stood near the edge of the bed watching him softly breathing into a pillow, his nude body spread-eagle, face down, across the Wedgewood blue satin sheets, the color of the sheets contrasting dramatically with his deeply tanned body. She smiled at his small rear end's cotton-tail whiteness.

Emma undressed, brushed her teeth, then slid across the cool satin sheets, snuggling against Tom's warm body. A few soft strokes across his back with her hand showed little promise of awakening him, and she instantly fell into a deep sleep. Her last thoughts were of Valentino and the same jumbled confusion: How could she possibly have had sex with an apparition? Did it really happen? Of course it had happened. Why?

Emma and Tom slept through the late afternoon without once stirring to eat or use the bathroom.

The early evening found them dripping with perspiration after sex. Thomas Glass was very much like his brother Travis. He preferred a fantasy world of sex in which women were dominant. Tom's whole-hearted participation and obsession in sports had been a govern on his hyperactivity and a block from becoming a full-fledged satyr, and even more so than his brother, Tom greatly enjoyed kinky sex.

Tom reveled in pain and pleasure; his ultimate pleasure was being spanked with the flat side of a hair brush while laying across Emma's lap. He was also quite athletic and innovative in his sexual performance, rarely bothering with the missionary position. One of his favorite verses was: "Sticks and stones may break my bones, but whips and chains excite me!"

Emma was sure that the proclivity for unusual ruttings stemmed from the men's very strange mother and her rigid notions of punishment and child rearing.

She shuddered with thoughts of the men's mother, Corrina Glass, and then just as quickly erased Corrina from her mind, sometimes having no mother at all was better than having her as a mother. Oh, indeed it was, she thought!

Tom was a younger, more virile version of Travis, and it was a natural and necessary progression for the survivors to find comfort in each other's arms. Emma had almost been destroyed over

Travis's death, and Tom had been equally devastated by the loss of his big brother, his best buddy and backbone.

VALENTINO'S CURSE

Emma observed some of Travis's obvious characteristics in Tom: drop dead good looks, brain power, athletic muscular build, facial expressions, similar tastes in clothing and colors, similar speech patterns, and a propensity for learning.

The two men were almost duplicates, except for a few key differences; Travis, as a popular professor had three well received, scholarly books, and numerous published articles in international professional publications. He was also a greatly requested lecturer and a good fund raiser for the university.

Travis had been a genuine and respected intellectual. Tom bordered on being a dumb jock on the surface, but his grasp in making piles of money and successful investments bordered on brilliance. Tom had several famous exercise videos, had had four national exercise and think and grow rich cable television shows, and was a greatly requested sports banquet speaker. Both men were gentle, soft spoken and treated Emma as the only woman in their world. And both had loved her irrevocably.

The most important gift Tom had given to her beside intense love, was his ability to draw her out of her shell. He lined up classes in Chinese calligraphy, watercolor painting, and gardening, all of which she stayed with. All of these complimented her need for quiet-mind time, and she became quite proficient at them. The gardening had lead to a board seat for volunteering in fund raising at the Denver Botanical Gardens, and her Chinese calligraphy and water colors were usual crowd favorites at local art shows. Her gardening, in particular with several rare breeds of roses, caused neighbors and passerbys to offer kudos, plus being featured in several newspaper articles. With increased volunteer and charity work, she was able to funnel generous amounts of her personal fortune into several charities, and boost interest in other causes by using her society standing at fund raisers. Her favorite charities were battered women's shelters and runaway youth programs, as well as children's hospital wards. She even set up a special charity for homeless pets in the name of her Rhodesian Ridge Back, Molly.

Emma drew the line with Tom when it came to participating in recreation and sports. Tom was a fierce competitor in tennis, golf, and handball, but they came together in running, hiking and swimming. Tom was very much like his older brother in any type of competition, and she used to grit her teeth while watching them compete in brotherly athletic and business functions.

None the less, and in every way, Tom had been

good for Emma, pulling her back into a world without Travis. After six months with Tom, she was able to empty Travis's clothing closets, bureau drawers, and ended the nightly ritual of spraying Travis's cologne on bed sheets and pillows. She threw away the cologne saturated handkerchiefs that she had carried in her purses. With Tom's tenderness and silent direction, she commenced a new chapter in her life, happy for the reprieve and release. She was even able to enjoy a full night's sleep without drugs.

Emma padded down the back stairs to the kitchen, pleasantly exhausted from sex and drained from wrestling with her anger over Dr. Kohen's seeming indifference.

Deciding on Eggs Benedict, freshly squeezed orange juice and coffee, she commenced rattling through the kitchen cupboards and refrigerator. Tom had earned a breakfast in bed.

"Why did you get up so early?"

Emma jumped at Tom's husky voice.

"Well, you went back to sleep, and I was hungry--I knew you'd be hungry after that performance."

"My performance?" He smiled, almost laughing.

Tom pressed against her back while she buttered rye toast on the kitchen island counter. She could feel him against her buttocks, made more sensual through their silk robes.

"Don't, I'm cooking."

Tom whispered in her ear, "Why not?"

"Because I'm hungry. Look, it's almost ready, sit down, and eat while it's hot."

"Hot? I've got something hot."

Emma turned around and buried her face in his hard chest. Tom held her tightly in his arms while kissing her neck.

"I'll never understand how you can be ready to go, over and over again!"

"Practice honey. It's you. Haven't you ever heard of Kegels?" Tom saw the question on her face.

"Kegels are exercises for men that help achieve firmer, almost continuous erections, greater ejaculatory control and more powerful orgasms." He sounded like a text book quote. "I learned how to do these exercises when I went to the Costa Brava Spa seminar last summer. Just part of my education for training the good old boys of the company."

Somehow the kitchen did not seem to be the place to continue the discussion on sex.

"Sit down and let's eat."

She hummed while she continued cooking. She saw that Tom was deeply buried in the business page looking for quotes on his stocks, knowing habit would draw him to the sports page.

Emma was content with their relationship. They were actually developing deeper ties than she thought possible. The sex was good, actually great, and the old joke was, he took the garbage out too. He had proposed three times, and had meant it. She was strongly reticent over marrying her husband's brother, sure somehow it was taboo in polite society, and she was nervous over marrying a younger man- -granted a handsome, loving and wealthy man, but still younger.

She hummed louder as she focused her thoughts on cooking.

Emma knew she was close to bouncing off the walls; at first she decided it was the coffee, then remembered the coffee was decaffeinated.

A Colorado cornflower blue sky allowed the sunshine to innocently meander through loosely-woven, burlap kitchen curtains. Shadows penetrated the sun-swept Americana decorated kitchen, hanging then drifting along the areas of the stuccoed kitchen walls, and into dim corners where the sun-light refused to go.

She rubbed her eyes, attempting to remove a filmy cloud of sleep. After trying to focus her eyes she realized the distortion was in the room itself and not in her eyes.

Several blobs of transparent clouds continued their movement through the room, waving like dissolving ink blots in a moving container of water, refusing to lose its feeling of menace.

Her memory suddenly clicked in. The séance. The same kind of shadows! She froze in alarm while tightly clinching her jaw muscles. Tom was contentedly sipping from a mug of coffee, riveted to the sports page.

He suddenly looked up, catching Emma's panicked stare. "Something wrong baby?"

She heard her voice stutter, "No, just drank too fast."

Tom continued staring. He knew something was bothering her. "You sure you're all right?"

"The coffee was too hot." She was growing faint from panic. She anchored her eyes on the large kitchen wall clock in order to steady herself against a sudden surge of vertigo.

His eyes dropped back to the newspaper. Minutes later when Emma rose to load the dishes in the dishwasher, his eyes followed her movement. Tom could feel something had disturbed the static comfort of the morning. It was now chilly in the kitchen and although very warm-blooded, he tightly wrapped the silk kimono around his broad chest. He reached down to briskly rub circulation into his chilled feet with ice-cold hands.

Emma's voice cut through the room. "I need to talk." Before Tom could reply, she continued, "Let's go into the family room."

They went into the adjoining room and plopped simultaneously onto the enormous brown corduroy couch.

Gathering thoughts, Emma sputtered, "Please don't think I'm nuts, but Tom...."

"He interrupted, hey, you know me better than that."

Emma felt a rush of reassurance with his quick reply. Tom had never once challenged her whims or moods. As a matter of fact, they had always been totally supportive of each other. No questions asked, no challenges issued. She smiled with memories of their big sister, little brother talks when she had first been engaged, then married to Travis.

She would have married Tom at the drop of a hat a year after Travis's death, except for one thing. Her intuition, that sixth sense that had faithfully guided her through difficult situations, warned her that marriage with Tom should not be forced until the signs were right. At this particular point in her life, Emma was not willing to compromise her hard earned independence and reputation. Knowing her wide circle of friends and acquaintances suspected she and Tom were more than a hot number--and if you didn't broadcast it, everybody would look the other way. It was the polite thing to do as some of them also had liaisons to hide.

"Come on, Em, I'm a grown up. Tell me. What's wrong?" Tom thought a little humor should be injected into the moment.

Emma haltingly told Tom about the séance, Valentino and the fantasized night she had spent with him. She retraced the story by underlining the incidents of the strong scent of fragrances in the house, the rose on the pillow, her grandmother's occupation and Other World gifts, and Valentino's magnificent slave bracelet.

Tom hung on every word without interjecting questions into her narrative. Emma looked deeply into his blue eyes, noticing intense concentration was now giving him a wild-eyed look.

"I don't know what to say, except wow!" Tom looked into the coffee mug while swallowing heavily, only pausing to thwart choking. "Do you feel you're in trouble?"

"I don't think so, not now anyway, but I can tell you this...I feel something is being set in motion; I can't put my finger on it, but it's like the beginning of a play, and I'm waiting in the wings for the cue to bring me to center stage."

Tom burst out, "Goddamn, just think of it, life after death! And you've seen it! Just think Em, it might be true. My God! Maybe you even did have sex with a ghost, this Valentino guy!"

Before she could respond, her eyes were attracted to the large antique colonial brass weather vane sitting on the marble topped coffee table. Tom's eyes followed hers.

A copper angel with a trumpet in its mouth, perched on top of a weather vane, was furiously spinning in 360 degree circles.

Tom jumped off the couch, knowing now what had made him uneasy. "Let's get dressed! We'll talk about this later. How about a walk in Washington Park and a shopping spree at the Cherry Creek Mall? Maybe a movie. I have to buy the new Masong exercise video and book anyway. Hurry, let's get dressed, I want to get out of here for a while!"

He walked over to Emma who was now almost

hypnotized by the angel's movement, helping her up from the couch--actually pulling her from the couch.

"We'll feel better in the sunshine of the park...and the flower gardens, and kids playing and laughing at the playground...and other living things. This shit is too heavy for us to deal with right now!"

They dressed and were out of the house in less than twenty minutes.

Transparent shapes hugged the ceiling, silent and observing, blending into the shadows of the room, watchful as Tom and Emma scrambled out of the house. Not choosing to follow the living, especially into cleansing sunshine, they were absorbed into the walls, taking their menace with them. They would return later.

Emma and Tom spent the remainder of the morning strolling hand-in-hand in the warm sunshine and flower gardens surrounding the two lakes of Washington Park, and the better part of the afternoon in the money-crush of the up-scale Cherry Creek mall.

Tom remained quiet and introspective, always smiling. When he felt Emma drifting away in thought, he would tightly squeeze her hand, kiss her on the cheek, or rub her shoulders.

Emma seemed to sleep walk through much of the day and several times was startled to find where Tom had led her.

Tom picked up the exercise video and book, spending an additional $570 for Polo shorts and tops in the Ralph Lauren shop, later buying Emma a very expensive black pearl scatter pin and matching earrings at Mountain-Park Jewelers.

Her mind continued operating full tilt beneath her sonambulence, her brain methodically attempting to sort out the past few days, outlining and organizing thoughts into some sort of cohesive file. She felt that deductive and inductive reasoning could lay out any problem into a precise schematic for any solution. Or she would have to revert to the unscientific approach, her intuition, and her great grandmother's legacy of clairvoyance and prophecy. For most of her life, Emma knew she had the 'Sight' which had been buried deep in her subconscious and rejected as foreign and strange. Emma had been terrified when she had first discovered these latent abilities.

At the last foster home she had been dumped

into and the ninth since she had been orphaned, the family had appeared average and 'normal' except for one thing: the lascivious looks and attention she received from the lumbering teenage son, pointed to potential problems, which eventually happened.

During the first meal she had with the Dunham family, Emma felt troubling vibrations directed at her, and looking up from her plate she caught the pig-eyes of Conrad Dunham and his thoughts. She excused herself and went to her bedroom.

Two years prior to the Dunham family, strange 'feelings' had entered her psyche and then had grown in intensity and power.

Sensations of chills would softly caress her hands then race up and down her back. There would be a tingling sensation in her palms and finger tips, and then a sudden rush of electrical-like currents would start racking her body. Soon spider web sensations would caress her face, setting off a wave of prickles.

In a matter of moments she knew she was prepared for something, but not knowing what the something was, she waited in anticipation. Her excitement grew.

If she closed her eyes she could see a montage of colored moving pictures. Most of the time she was unsure of what the jumbled pictures meant.

VALENTINO'S CURSE

The night Conrad entered her bedroom she had not been surprised. She heard his heavy breathing while he was thinking of her. She also was prepared.

The noise from his mind chatter grew louder as he neared her room, and the closer he drew, her fear galvanized into a surge of kinetic energy.

Her bedroom was lit with a swirling white blur of light and energy that first floated above her, then slowly entered her prone body. She waited breathlessly for Conrad to enter her room.

Emma could see the powerful hulk of the young man standing in what he thought was the security of the inky-black bedroom, clad only in white under shorts that revealed his excitement.

Her heart was pounding hard as he drew closer. She recoiled when he bent over her.

At first he softly caressed her body with his muscular hands, which quickly went out of control when he commenced squeezing her budding breasts.

She could see the flash of energy arc from her body and enter into his hands. Conrad groaned, but was unable to cry out when the searing pain slammed throughout his body. He ran from the room.

The three years she spent with the Dunham family resulted in the most peaceful foster home she had known. Conrad grew to respect her emerging womanhood and her privacy; they even became quasi-friends. There was never a mention of what had happened.

With that night ending in resolution, the power of Emma's abilities were pushed back into her subconscious, but never completely.

She found that by relaxing then clearing her mind, she was able to hear people's thoughts. She was also able to assimilate words and thoughts in every book she read, which obviously assisted her becoming a top honor student in the schools she entered.

"Let's go see a movie, the movie about Australia and the outback, the one with the beauty and the wolf man, or whatever he is, something like that--stop laughing, you know which one I'm talking about, well, it's leaving this weekend."

Emma laughed at Tom's puckered expression and he countered: "How about stopping at Bendetto's Pizzaria, taking a Kitchen Sink special home, and watching the two movies we just got from the video mail club?"

"Sure, sounds good."

She was relieved with Tom's quick agreement for two reasons, she was exhausted, and was damned if she was going to let 'them' drive her out of her own home.

She could easily read Tom's thoughts and for once, sex was not foremost in his mind, he was strangely fearful of the house and in a confrontation with what they might discover.

Emma fought her ability to read minds. She remembered the time Travis died. She would never forget the moment when his final cry of anguish ripped through her brain. She knew it was his last gasp of breath, his life force smothered in suffocation; she read pinpricks of his thoughts and shared his pain.

In an early Saturday afternoon three years ago, she was hosting a tea for the university library women's guild. Laughing over a risque joke, Travis's thoughts suddenly tore into her brain like hot rivets. She sprang from her chair and collapsed, falling across two seated women. With that incident, she at last became a reluctant believer in her latent abilities.

She waited that long afternoon with Donna for the dreaded telephone call she knew would come, almost passing out after consuming several glasses of straight Scotch and smoking two packages of cigarettes. The call came three days later.

Tom's essence, unlike Travis's, was totally sexual and athletic in nature. His employment as a popular and much in demand athletic trainer to the gigantic high-tech, MentaMax Corporation, and as the personal trainer and health consultant to the CEO and chief corporate officers and board members, attested to his athletic skills and personality.

His yearly income from being a health and jock guru in the corporation was in the high six figures, additional income sweetened by national sales of three ghost-written exercise books with companion videos.

Tom's type A mind was singular in approach. Hard work equaled money, lots of money, all channeled into investment portfolios. His economic well-being was derived from a healthy body and vibrant mental outlook which lead to guilt free frequent sex with just about every woman he met. He could have been classified as a male slut, that was, until he fell head over heals in love with Emma, especially when his brother landed her, and he knew when to back off and get a grip on his feelings. Emma became his excuse for weaning himself from sleeping with every woman he met and learning how to be chaste, not a saint but an individual who truly respected himself and the many women he met.

Now, again "it" happened; it came back and Tom was confounded and a little more than frightened with the thought of confrontation with the unknown. It had happened once before, big time. He instinctively knew what Emma had told him was true and also what she hadn't said, Now he had to find the answers to what entities had visited the house. He was damned afraid again. Tom had reason to be.

Chapter 6

They were hesitant in entering the house. Tom feigned interest in the front lawn, stooping several times to pull out dandelions. Emma pawed through the trunk of the BMW for the shopping bags.

They stood looking at each other, waiting for the other to make the first move. Emma finally took the initiative.

"What in the heck are we afraid of?" Quickly adding, "I'm not going to be driven out of my home by a bunch of imagined spooks or whatever in the hell they are!"

Tom screwed up his courage, "I'll go in first." He unlocked the front door, and without hesitation, leaped into the foyer, almost slipping and breaking his neck on the marble parquet floor. Emma followed him closely.

They spent the better part of an hour searching each room, and then finding nothing, Emma

VALENTINO'S CURSE

charged into the kitchen and put a kettle of water on the stove for tea.

Tom pointed at the telephone. "It looks like the answering machine is going crazy."

She looked at the machine sitting on the breakfast room counter. The display indicator showed eighteen messages, the small red light blinking with dyspepsia. She made a mental note again to switch to voice mail.

Emma's neck hair stood on end with a terse message from Donna Epstein. Karl Michael had committed suicide. Jack Sewell had discovered his body hanging in their garage.

She called Donna several times, frustrated with no answer, she left a message.

Karl could not shake the feeling of being watched. For the first time ever, he locked the bathroom door before taking a shower. While he was shaping his beard in the bathroom mirror he had the distinct feeling that something was staring over his shoulder. He was so nervous that he accidentally clipped too much hair from the left side of his beard.

Karl was sure his growing agitation was coming from the luncheon interview he was about to have with a reporter that he thoroughly despised. He always resolved to meet conflicts head on, even when it came to the news media.

Ever since he had become a national celebrity through a controversial television talk show, the local press had hounded him for interviews. He hated interviews for one reason, knowing they were after one thing, his public humiliation for expounding the importance of contact with the after life. Then again, he was relieved to be getting out of the house which had been getting on his nerves lately—and strangely.

Jack Sewell, his six year long lover, partner and assistant, had spent the last two days in Boulder with his sick brother and was due to return in the evening.

He felt nervous and unsettled. The house was uncomfortably cool for the late morning, and a sickeningly sweet fragrance of flowers managed to penetrate his infected sinuses, the odor he assumed, came from the back yard rose garden.

Sneezing twice, he struggled out of a black leather sling chair, going to the tissue box sitting on top of the stereo speakers. He sneezed again.

Karl had delayed his leaving for the Buffalo Grille, a five block walk from his house on Denver's

VALENTINO'S CURSE

Capitol Hill district. It felt good knowing the reporter would be squirming, wondering if he would be stood up; no use in throwing himself immediately into the breech.

After shutting and locking the windows on the first floor he made his way to the front door, pausing to look at a tablet on the hall table which held the electronic combination to the recently installed burglar alarm system. He couldn't remember what he had done with his cell phone, probably had left it in his car.

Karl's sparse hair stood on end. He turned, facing the living room. Four transparent shapes floated into the room. His instinctive call for protection from the White Light was not in time.

He knew who they were and why they had come, actually surprised they had taken this long to show up. Karl had always been prepared to meet his demise, but he was mildly annoyed that it had to be over such a trivial discovery and on their terms.

They grabbed him in an ice-cold embrace. The last thing he remembered was his right hand being forced to write on a pad of paper, and then being picked up and floated on his back through the living room into the garage.

A coil of yellow nylon cord used for tying

camping equipment to the top of the Jeep was put around his neck in split seconds, and while his final tears of regret and fear were dribbling down his cheeks, he could feel warm urine soaking his trousers, and agonizing pain as his brain and body functions ceased.

Whenever Emma was distraught, she would head for the kitchen and cook. Since she had not made the normal Saturday morning run to Silver's Park Avenue Grocery Store, she dug through the garage freezer then the refrigerator in the kitchen. The pizza they had brought home the other night did not now seem appropriate for dinner. She slid the pizza box back into the refrigerator.

The shock of Karl's suicide permeated her thoughts. True, she had barely known him, but in two meetings she recognized a kindly man. A person that could have assisted her in establishing contact with Travis. A man that would have been important in her life: he had the knowledge she had been seeking.

She dabbed at her eyes with a paper towel, then softly blew her nose. She put on the teapot, made four toasted cheese sandwiches and micro-waved a large carton of frozen French fries. She put the food on a serving tray and carried it to the living room.

Tom was engrossed in an oversized book, not once looking up when she silently glided into the room.

"What are you reading? I don't remember that book."

Tom said, "I bought it at the mall today, don't you remember? It's a book on the history of silent movies; it has a thick chapter on Valentino's life. Very interesting information about our boy...and some very strange facts."

Tom's comments chilled her. Valentino's visit to her bed—if it had happened, continued to linger in her mind. She went into the kitchen to telephone Donna, which was again unsuccessful.

They spent the rest of the evening trying to relax. Tom silently rereading the chapter on Valentino while sipping strong, black tea and eating most of the sandwiches and fries. Emma sat staring at the oil painting of the ocean near Malibu she had bought Travis on their vacation in California five years ago.

Tension made her yawn until she closed her mouth at the sound of her jaws popping. Frustration laced with depression straddled her back and shoulders like a one-hundred pound sack of cement.

Karl Michael's death, followed by their early morning home visit from less than friendly spirits, or something sinister, had sucked at her reservoir of energy. She knew Karl's passing would inevitably involve her, the reasoning being that nothing ever occurred by chance in spiritual matters. She shuddered at the thought, intuitively feeling she was somehow responsible for his death and thereby putting some force in motion. Guilt feelings again over not being more pro-active when she could?

Tom's voice interrupted her thoughts. "Honey, I said that I know you're exhausted, but could I see Valentino's slave bracelet before we turn in?"

Tom walked to Emma while holding the opened movie book, using one hand as a pointer.

"Our hero."

Emma looked at the picture of the handsome, olive-skinned Italian lover standing in front of a swimming pool. He was dressed in a modest one piece bathing suit that covered his torso and hips. She appraised the lithe figure and face of the silent movie star, having a good idea of why he had attracted the lust of so many collapsed libidos in the Nineteen-twenties.

"Well, how about that" Tom pointed at Valentino's left wrist in the sultry picture. "Do you see it?"

Emma looked, knowing exactly what he was referring to. Valentino was wearing the slave bracelet. The intricate links were exactly the same.

"Yes, that's it."

"You're sure?"

"From what I read in my great grandmother's diary...yes, I know I have it. And don't forget the vibrations from the bracelet, the reason why Karl Michael decided to hold the sitting, no, no mistake." She felt a twinge of nausea.

"Could I read your great grandmother's diary?"

"It's somewhere in the basement. We can look for it later." Tom said, "let's turn in. For some reason I feel beaten-up."

They walked arm in arm up the stairs to the master bedroom. Tom shed his clothes on the floor in seconds. Emma modestly undressed in her changing closet. She smoothed out the peach satin nightgown's wrinkles, feeling the contours of her slight hips and the ripeness of her taught breasts. She was pleased with her sensual figure which still managed to illicit comments.

Tom sprawled across the bed clad in a pair of maroon silk boxer shorts. He was lying on his stomach deeply engrossed in the movie book. He heard the rustle of her satin nightgown.

"It seems that our prince of love and the pack he ran with were very much involved in the spirit world. He had a spirit guide called Black Feather. Here, look. This hokey picture shows him dressed like his Indian guide. And look at this one. Don't laugh, it's supposed to be a photograph of Valentino in the after life!"

Emma looked over his shoulder at the photograph. She was thinking how a modern day reader would undoubtedly chuckle at the poorly doctored picture. Weeks ago she would have smiled at the photograph, but with Valentino's abrupt entry into her life, she frowned.

"Don't turn out the lights yet, I want to read some more." Tom continued, "Can I see the slave bracelet?"

She groaned under her breath, not really wanting to think about the paranormal at bedtime. She went to the four-drawer jewelry box sitting on the corner of the marble topped vanity table, opening the top drawer. She could feel the vibrations pulsating from the gleaming metal, which also radiated a glowing fire-red color.

She dropped it in his open palm.

"Sonafabitch! It's hot!" Tom slammed it on the bed like he had been burned.

"Honey, pick it up, would you?"

Emma leaned over the bed and scooped up the heavy gold bracelet and said, "See it doesn't burn me. And it didn't burn Donna when she took it to the séance, which is kind of strange."

"Can you do that psychometry thing?"

"Not now. I've done enough for today. I'm tired."

"Only one last question--what was it like to be uh, bedded by Valentino? How did he feel, uh, you know what I mean."

"Jesus! What do you think? I didn't ask to have a spirit rape me, and besides, I don't really know if it happened at all."

"I'm sorry Em, I can be a real ass. Please, I'm sorry. Forgive me?"

"Yes, but it was a stupid question." She smiled, "However, he could never compare to you, even if alive."

Tom turned out the lights and held her in his arms, nuzzling her cheek with his lips.

"Are we alone, Em?"

She knew he was only half joking, but Emma felt a sudden chill with the recall of the shadows and the spinning angel on the weathervane.

"They're gone, at least for the time being." She knew they would return.

She was on the bottom rim of sleep, but without enough control to wake up, and not enough in command to plunge into the chasm.

Emma dreamt a collage of moving pictures. She saw Valentino, Karl Michael, and his hanging from the garage rafters, clear enough to make her believe that she had been there. Travis, and something in a dark hooded robe--she could not make out the face, standing at the foot of the bed. She saw herself wearing the slave bracelet while watching sunshine bounce off the shimmering gold.

She woke at six o'clock. A soft breeze gently stirred the bedroom sheers. Emma stretched, hearing her neck bones gently pop. Tom's sleepy eyes watched her.

"Good morning beautiful." Tom pulled her tightly to his left side. He gently stroked her breasts. The sensation through her satin nightgown caused her nipples to stand hard.

Tom took her right hand to his mouth, gently biting each finger. His lips, then tongue, covered her right ear, neck and cheeks.

She was ready. The tension of the previous day tightly knotted her body. She helped Tom's hurried removal of the nightgown over her head, impatient with his slowness.

Tension finally released it's strangle hold through multiple orgasms; sexual exhaustion sent its desired release.

Chapter 7

They left the house for Sunday breakfast at the Harvest Cafe. It had been Travis's favorite Sunday breakfast place because of the freshly squeezed, pulpy orange juice and Maine blueberry pancakes. Now it was the only breakfast place where she and Tom went.

One side of the rustic, brick-walled restaurant held racks of Colorado Sunday newspapers liberalized with newspapers from the East and West Coasts. She had always marveled at how the restaurant was able to get the newspapers overnight in time for Sunday morning.

Emma knew Tom was about to make one of his Sunday reflections. He had surprised her several times with thoughts and events that he rarely spoke about. She once had classified Tom as a gentleman jock, kinky lover and intellectually as exciting as a rock. As she had come to realize that he was much deeper in intellect and interests, she had been delighted with numerous discoveries.

"Em, bear with me. Do you remember the time when I disappeared for over three years, and Travis and you thought I had gone to Europe with Jennifer Springs? Well, heck, I didn't. God, this is going to be hard, it'll make sense, I promise. Well, I was in Nevada, in prison...for supposed drug dealing."

Tom held Emma's riveted attention. She saw the intensity in Tom's eyes.

"After I was paroled, only getting out of the joint because they needed bed space, I hit the skids...even worse. Man, was I at a low point, the worst I've ever been in my entire life. Dealing, stealing, prostitution, anything to get the stuff. I Had this gun I'd stolen from a break-in, and found myself in a back alley in Vegas, and alone. I couldn't call Travis or you. Hell, I was a loser. A real loser! You have no idea how low a man could fall. I shoved the gun barrel into my mouth and was counting down the seconds from ten, when 'He' came."

"Who came?" She swallowed hard.

"The Messenger...'Him'. Please bear with me, let me talk it out. This guy was dressed in a black shirt and black pants. Long black hair, he had unbelievable white shining teeth. Good looking in a strange way. Early thirties. He glowed, Em, glowed with a violet and red-colored fog that almost covered him...

maybe it came from him, I don't know, but it was really weird."

Emma stopped him and nervously ordered more coffee. She needed a break from the intensity of Tom's narration. She knew this revelation was hard for him to talk about. Tom gulped down an entire glass of water, sputtering and coughing with tension. He held the cloth napkin to his mouth while he continued his coughing.

"Something he did--I don't know what, made me drop the gun, it was like he was talking in my head, anyway I heard the gun fall in the alley. He held my head in his hands because I tried to look away from his eyes. Damn, I can still see them. Brilliant copper-brown eyes. Em, he never said a word, yet I heard him. I don't know...it was damn confusing. Honey, he warned me about taking my own life. He was some sort of messenger, no, a 'warner'. It seems these warners, confront troubled people and others who've lost hope. It's the first and only warning a person ever gets! If you don't follow their advice... then some sort of an angel of death takes you. I swear that's what I picked up. He was all I needed to get back on track! The job I have now, he got for me, I think...didn't know that did you? I've been clean, good, ever since, only bad habit was bedding women! Let's eat and I'll tell you more later, okay?" Tom was shaking.

Emma was stunned with his revelation. She knew Tom well enough to believe him. She had few doubts about anything now, especially after what had recently rolled over her.

Her mind wandered while she watched him eat. Her appetite had vanished while her mind was busy categorizing and arranging events into bite-sized, digestible pieces.

Tom looked up from his plate and met her eyes, he was obviously going to continue; she knew he had to continue now that he had unleashed his thoughts.

"He had a name, and even though I know he was--is, a supernatural being with absolutely no malice, to this day, to this very minute, I still look over my shoulder. What is strange, really strange, is that I can't remember what his face looked like...it's almost like part of my memory was erased. I don't do drugs, very seldom drink, and never try to hurt anyone. I know I could be taken whenever they feel I don't cut it."

They looked at each other. Silence was appropriate because neither knew what to say.

Finally Emma spoke. "Tom, I haven't a clue,

I don't know what to say. I certainly don't doubt what you went through, or that this messenger came to you. I just don't understand why, or how, these things happen. There are no logical explanations that fit. You know me well enough to know that I never make snap judgments."

She reached across the table and held his shaking, cold hands.

"I do love you. I don't like being out of control, you of all people, know how I hate not being able to control events, but there is nothing we can do about it. This situation is beyond us. I think we're on the edge of something about to happen, something that might let us live more in hope and less in fear."

When they got home Emma went to the answering machine to see if Donna had returned her calls. Donna had left two messages, the last message at 11:18.

Donna snapped, "Where in the hell have you been?"

Emma was taken back by the anger in Donna's voice. Before she could reply, Donna again snapped.

"Well, as you already know, Karl was found

hanging in the garage. Jack said it was horrible! I won't go into the morbid details. I went over to their house, of course after the body was removed, and I spent the night holding Jack's hand. Well, guess what? Karl had left a note. All it said was: 'What is illusion and what is real?' Jack and I read the note over and over again, but couldn't figure out what he meant. Jack also failed to tell the police about the note, so don't say anything, Em, Hell, what's the harm, have you ever heard of the police ever solving anything? Why are you so quiet?"

Emma was exasperated. "Because, I haven't have a chance to get a word in edge wise. Don't pick on me, this is horrible!"

Donna went on, ignoring Emma's statement. "Then here's another shocker. Do you remember that stud policeman at the séance? Robert Shell? Get this. He's the investigating detective. He'll be talking to all of us, so expect him to see you. I don't know how he'll have the time to talk to the hundred or so members of the church, but that's his problem. He's one of us anyway...like you're one of us."

Emma cut in. "One of us?"

"My dear, of course you're one of us. You may not know it yet, but Karl did and Jack does. Jack's going to talk with you as soon as he gets control of himself, I think he said after Karl's memorial service. He's being cremated early next week, which allows him to completely sever his silver cord, his tie, from his earthly body. You will be invited to the séance to contact him. Jack is going to wait the two weeks so that Karl can adjust to the other side. I've got to go. Call me tomorrow, and Em, don't forget that Detective Shell will be seeing you. Oh, I forgot! It wasn't suicide."

"What do you mean it wasn't suicide, Donna?"

"To kill yourself is the ultimate sin. Breaking a contract with the universe. If you do, the chances are probable that you will stay an earth-bound entity, a spook, a haunter, maybe forever. Karl believed in this very strongly. Em, he didn't commit suicide. Sorry dear, there's another call on the line. Call you later. kisses."

She was stunned. Karl murdered? If Karl did not kill himself, then who did? She wanted to tell Tom, but remembered he was out on his daily six mile run. She shook her head over Donna's matter-of-fact statements and her seeming lack of compassion over Karl's death. She thought it was cold on Donna's part, something she had never experienced before from her friend.

When Tom returned from running they took a

shower together. The sex was as hot as the water shooting from three shower heads that licked their bodies.

Tom remained speechless about Karl's death. Emma knew it had shaken him, especially when she told him about Donna's conversation. She did not solicit his comments.

Later that afternoon, she made a dinner of salad, grilled Porterhouse steaks and baked potatoes. After eating, they snuggled on the family room couch and watched a mindless comedy on cable that was stupid enough for them to laugh hard, and enough for them to momentarily forget Karl's horrible death.

After the movie they slipped into their routine of drinking freshly ground coffee and reading. It was their way of gently easing from the weekend into preparation for blue Monday.

Tom would go to his ten hour plus job at the corporate head office in the Denver Tech Center, and Emma would help with the organizing and pricing of the books for the yearly university book sale, and several board meetings.

She would never have to work again if she chose not to, but also knew she would return to the world of work in the capacity of an associate anthropology professor. She had almost two months left on her leave of absence, time enough to wait while a new grant was being arranged for her defunct position. As soon as this problem with Valentino and these so-called spirits was concluded, if at all, she would return to her teaching job. Enough time had expired for her grieving. With Karl's passing and the terrible way he died was arrived at, perhaps concluded, she was sure that everything would start coming together again.

Shell's visit and the memorial service for Karl Michael seemed to arrive at warp speed.

The cremation was on Tuesday, the memorial service held on Thursday afternoon, with over three hundred friends and the curious packing the church. Jack Sewell was in excellent form, actually getting the assembly to break into tasteful applause when he talked about the "life" that surely would be waiting Karl when he completed his entry through the portals of eternity. He had completed an Earth life well lived with a great adventure awaiting his new spirit.

The final round of applause was over Jack's promise of an eternity for everyone, that is, for those who did the right unselfish and loving things in this life, and for those who believed in an afterlife.

Emma hung on Jack's every word. Tom watched Emma dabbing at her tears several times with a lace bordered handkerchief. Jack's promise of an afterlife was offered through the Spiritualist steps of meditation, séances, specific esoteric literature and belief.

Tom was consumed with thoughts on the prospects of eternity. He also hoped that he was continuing to fulfill the unwritten contract of the messenger. He applauded along with the congregation when the ushers removed the canistered ashes of Karl Michael from the white and gold painted column sitting at the foot of the altar.

Police Detective Robert Shell stood at Emma's door that Friday night. She was keenly annoyed with his intrusion at first, but then remembered Donna's warning that he would be coming for information on Karl's death.

She still swore under her breath. It was the inconvenience of the visit on a Friday evening. Friday was her bridge night. Four couples had been involved with round-robin bridge at each other's homes for several years and she hated a break in this treasured routine.

"Don't you believe in calling in advance?"

"I'm sorry Mrs. Glass. Just forgot. I frequently

get so involved in my busy schedule that I forget the protocol of having my secretary call yours."

Emma felt a quick flash of guilt at Shell's sarcasm. He was only trying to do his job. She felt annoyed with herself over turning it into a petty situation.

Robert Shell was darkly handsome, weighing approximately 210 muscular pounds tightly packed on a six foot-four inch frame. Intelligence radiated from his unusual copper-brown eyes as did a sense of invincibility. He was not a man to push around.

Emma felt like a jaded, silly-willed girl next to his mature and courtly manner.

"Please excuse my rudeness Mr. Shell, for a few minutes I felt put out. I know why you're here, what happened, and I must tell you that I know nothing; I mean, I don't see how I could possibly contribute to the investigation. Please come in." She felt stupid with her nervous chatter.

Emma led the way to the study. She offered him coffee and a chair. He declined both.

"I'll be brief because of your guests. I know you had nothing to do with Karl Michael's death, but I must warn you to be on guard. They might be after all of us."

"Who will be after us...oh, do you mean?" She almost said shadows. She stared upward into his handsome face. Copper-brown eyes set in a classical Greek face, like the Hermes sculpture she had seen on a tour of Athens. He radiated. He glowed. She shook her head slightly trying to shake the clouds away from her vision, and the trembling in her knees and the strange tickle in her solar plexus.

She thought it, he said it.

"He did not commit suicide. No chair or stool to kick-off from. The noose was hung much too high from the rafters for him to perform a 9.0 gymnastic routine."

Emma knew what he was going to say next.

"They did it. Several of our spirit friends took him, and hanged him. They made him suffer. I suspect he was close to some sort of discovery that I'm not aware of, as yet. I want to warn you again. Please protect yourself and Tom with the White Light which offers some protection. Do you understand me? I will leave my card in anticipation of meeting with you next week, at your convenience of course, so we can talk a few things over." His eyes bore into hers. She knew that he was genuinely concerned.

She led him to the front door. Watching his powerful silhouette disappear into the night, Emma leaned heavily against the door frame while his car drove away, then rejoined her guests.

Chapter 8

The week sprinted by. Tom was involved in instructing five corporation athletic trainers in the treatment of weekend athletic injuries. Exhausted every night, he collapsed into bed forgoing eating, conversation and sex.

Emma on the other hand, slogged through the week, waiting for telltale signs announcing the return of the specters; she felt Valentino could be dealt with, but the spirits were another matter.

On Wednesday, Donna's housekeeper had tersely informed Emma that Donna had abruptly flown to New York on Tuesday; Emma became further stressed, another recent snap decision which ran counter to Donna's well-planned scheduling. Emma knew that something was amiss, but then she had given up long ago trying to divine what Donna did.

And when Detective Shell had failed to return her telephone calls, She felt an additional burr had been jammed under her saddle. All in all, she was skittish and off balance during the week.

The annual Denver University book sale, this year held for two days at one of suburban Denver's largest shopping malls, had set a record in sales. The guild committee decided to hold an impromptu celebration Thursday night at the chancellor's house for the guild volunteers.

Robert Shell walked out the back entrance of the chancellor's Tudor mansion, pausing on the staircase landing while he scrutinized the well-dressed crowd milling in the garden and lawn.

Emma's back was turned to the mansion while she chatted with a group of friends while downing a third Vodka martini.

She felt a charge of electricity shoot through the back of her head, with sharp prickles of heat spreading across her upper back; the discomfort wrenched her attention to the mansion.

At first she thought one of her periodic migraines had taken life. When she turned, her eyes caught the shape of a tall man standing in the shadows near the mansion's back entrance. Despite the inky darkness of the moonless night, the only light coming from

Japanese lanterns strung haphazard above the garden lawn, she knew who the man was.

Shell! Rattled at knowing where she was, she quickly brushed his appearance aside. Of course, he was a police detective and had probably been told by Tom where she was. Emma dropped her confusion...did it really matter one way or the other?

He was also reading her mind. She struggled to fend his mind probes away, but his bombardment was much stronger than her block.

She watched him stride toward her while she calmly sipped her drink.

"Hello Mrs.Glass."

"Good evening detective."

"Please, Robert, remember, we know each other." In the same breath he continued. "Tom told me where you were. Sorry I didn't respond to your messages before this. You look lovely tonight."

Emma blushed. "Thank you for the compliment. Are you trying to flatter me?"

"No, just stating a fact. If you weren't seeing Tom, I'd be giving you the rush. Your black velvet dress frames your beauty."

She lost her reserve and blushed again. She was caught off guard by a sincere, masculine compliment.

Shell hesitated, "I've talked to everyone that remotely knew Karl, but I've drawn blanks. Can you help me?"

"Let's not play games. You stated before that he was murdered by spirit forces. You and I both know it's a fact, so you're not really that disappointed in drawing a blank. Also, you amaze me. How on earth could you possibly interrogate everyone that knew Karl in such a short period of time?"

"I have my ways as you are more than aware. Emma, do you honestly believe that I can put my real findings and suspicions into an official police report?"

Emma backed away from Shell. He was completely surrounded by an aura of pulsating, violet light.

Shell startled at her abrupt backward step. "What's wrong?"

"I can see it! Your aura."

He moved closer to her, whispering, "You can see my aura?"

"Robert, no more games. Why on earth would a detective be in a séance group, know about spirit forces, be adroit at mind reading, and whatever else I can only guess at."

He laughed. "Why respond? You obviously

VALENTINO'S CURSE

know a few of the answers. I can't tell you much at this point except that I am a genuine Denver police detective investigating a suicide--correction, murder, and I've developed a few psychic powers in the process. What else can I say?"

Emma was again flustered. She knew he was telling her a smattering of truth, she also knew he was not going to tell her anything else.

"Then why did you really come here tonight? You already warned me, remember?"

He paused, looking around to make sure they were not overheard. "To tell you about my investigation will not reveal anything, and to again warn you to be on your guard...."

She interrupted. "That again. On guard from what?"

"We both know that something is about to happen, and I really don't want you to be the next victim."

"Next victim? Why me?"

"I honestly don't know. I have a hunch you are at the center of whatever is building. Hell, I can't connect the dots yet. Jack Sewell has had a series of dreams about our group. He thinks his dreams are coming from Karl. In any case, Jack knows he's in danger, and you too. I don't want to unduly alarm you, but Tom's life is now in jeopardy."

"Tom?" Her heart skipped a beat.

"Yes. Tom might know something he hasn't shared. Emma, he has a highly developed talent for clairvoyance, a little untested at the moment, but he has the sight, nonetheless. Well, anyway, Jack says the recent problems have something to do with Valentino, but he can't quite grasp what it is. Jack wants you to invite Tom to the Saturday night séance."

"What séance? I wasn't informed about a Saturday séance. Isn't it presumptuous to assume that I'll be there? I only went to the last one because Donna dragged me there. I really don't think I'm interested in participating in another one!" She was gritting her teeth so much that her jaw hurt.

She was angry, realizing that she was almost screaming at Shell when several people stopped their conversations and stared at them.

"Ah, the real reason why I'm here. You must come. Emma, you possibly hold the key to this mess. Please think about it and please ask Tom to come. I can't take no for an answer. It's important. Excuse my bluntness, but you will be there. We are counting on you!"

To thwart a refusal, Shell spun around and briskly walked to the mansion. Emma watched him leave.

She was awed at the power of his aura which appeared to light up the darkness with a now luminous, neon purple color. She fleetingly wondered how many people in the garden were psychic enough to see the light.

Tom snapped his cell phone shut and faced Emma, obviously annoyed: "Jack was rather insistent on my being at the Saturday night sitting. He says we're to be at Donna's house tonight for a dress rehearsal and dinner for the special séance. I'm really not happy about doing this--you know how I feel about hocus pocus, goose chases!"

Emma was confused by the rapid tumble of events. Donna had flown to New York without informing her, a Saturday night séance, and now a Friday séance rehearsal with a dinner at Donna's home.

"I have to tell you Tom, I'm damned concerned over this sudden urgency of events. What's the problem--do you think?"

"Jack said that he has picked the most receptive and attuned sitters, those who have a direct interest in contacting Karl's spirit. This is developing into a real melodrama."

"I'm confused about you too, Tom. This thing about a mysterious person in a Las Vegas alley, and your total acceptance of spirit entities, like Valentino, and the rest of this hocus pocus--your words, has thrown me off balance, but it doesn't seem to really bother you at all--then Sewell and Shell's insistence on your attendance at the sitting--I'm missing something!" She was growing angry in her confusion.

"Em, what can I say? I told you some of the deep do-do that I went through, but I didn't tell you everything. I just can't, at least for now. Well, no bridge tonight. Do you call our friends, or should I?"

"I'll do it. I just hope all this damn stress won't bring on my migraines again. I hate the pain! I have three pills left and I refuse to see that damn shrink for another refill."

Tom sat on the couch with her. He took both her hands and brought them to his lips. "Babe, you know I love you. Believe me when I say your one fine woman. Everybody loves you, but no one more than me. I only wish you'd loosen up and stop being so hard on yourself. Your well-planned life can't continue. Obviously something is in the wind...even I can feel it. Nothing is ever going to be the same again. You've got to be stronger than you ever have, I'm just pissed off that all of this is happening at once!"

VALENTINO'S CURSE

"You know how much I love you Tom, but with Karl's death and Valentino's involvement, the spirits in the house, it's all starting to wear a little thin. I know one thing for sure, I won't agree to be the medium Saturday night. Besides, I don't know how, or want to know how."

Chapter 9

Emma remained quiet throughout the sumptuous six course dinner. As usual, Donna had outdone herself with the catered dinner and three male servers dressed in crisp black uniforms.

The formal table setting was enhanced with two large Waterford crystal vases filled with arrangements of white roses accented with baby's breath and green foliage. White candles flickered on the long dining table, causing muted light to bounce off the antique Belgian wall tapestries, turning the room into a Rembrandt-like stage set of shadows.

She looked at Donna several times but was unable to catch her eyes. Emma was still wondering about her hurried visit to New York, her quick reappearance, and the hosting of an extravagant sit-down dinner.

Jack Sewell interrupted the lively table conversation at desert. "I would like to thank Donna for this magnificent dinner, and for allowing us to have the sitting tomorrow night at this lovely home."

Everyone looked at Donna while voicing their appreciation.

Donna stood up and with a flutter of her hands indicated the adjoining room. "Please follow me to the drawing room, where we'll have coffee."

Jack and Donna led the dinner party into the library. When they had entered the room, Donna closed the balanced cherry-wood sliding doors.

Emma sat with Tom on the Louis XVI settee next to the open French doors. A scented breeze wafted in from the rose garden, cooling the moisture on the back of her neck.

"A little light." Donna turned the dimmer switch to bright. The Austrian chandler hanging above the center of the room grew bright, temporarily blinding the expectant guests.

Jack spoke. "We are all interconnected in Karl's death, not to say we are anywhere responsible, of course, but somehow each of us holds a piece of the puzzle. To help us begin the solving of this puzzle, we are privileged to have a guest with us who will assist us in following the stringent guidelines for a controlled séance. Madame Domina Redmond of the United Kingdom, has graciously shortened her stay with New York friends to participate in our séance, and a very special break for us too, I might add."

Jack sat down when Domina Redmond stood up.

"I am delighted to be here, and despite the difficult circumstances, I am most pleased to join you at tomorrow's sitting."

Emma noticed the approval registered on Shell's face.

Madame Redmond looked directly at Emma and Tom. "I see two people here whom I have not met."

She effortlessly glided over to them. Tom stood up. She gently fluttered her hand to both of them in a brushing handshake.

Emma immediately felt an enormous surge of energy shoot through her body. She also discerned an aura of white and pulsating violet light surrounding Madame Redmond's body. She was not alone in seeing the powerful aura. Tom mumbled excitedly under his breath while the others in the room softly gasped. Emma was inwardly startled in the realization that Tom could see auras.

Madame Redmond glided to the center of the room.

Domina Redmond was short, prune-wrinkled, and her face and hands were prominently covered in liver spots. Her frail body was topped with dyed carrot-red hair that shocked her cherry-red dress into submission. The bright-green fire in her eyes emitted the take-charge bearing of a much younger person, and a very strong-willed woman. Her genuine smile and gregarious demeanor could light up any gathering.

Madame Redmond spoke in an upper-class English accent. "I was invited to be the medium, I assume because of my distance from this terrible situation, and perhaps because I also have been a medium for over sixty years. I discovered at an early age that I had the sight--I however, prefer the term, gift. I have never done readings for money, possibly because I've always been filthy rich."

Emma laughed with the others.

Madame Redmond continued. "We Spiritualists are laughed at, hounded by the police and scorned by the scientific community, yet we persist. Why? Because it is the very nature of our gift. We help others to reconcile their differences with the ultimate adventure, death. Persecution for our beliefs is a given. Human beings, along with every living thing on every planet and star in the cosmos of God's eye, are born to perish. Our mission, yes duty, is to lighten this load. To make it bearable. Think. What do we do when we die? Is this life all there is? We in this lovely room know better. Our controls or spirit guides, even our dearly departed, give us hints, and sometimes even haunt us."

She paused while she took several sips of water from a crystal tumbler that looked enormous in her frail hands. The room was quiet while everyone mulled over what she had said.

"It is our duty to bring to others the knowledge of what we know about eternity, and to inform them that the other side can be one of growth and happiness. As I said before, we all will undergo some sort of persecution for our beliefs, but we also will join a distinguished multitude of Spiritualists who have gone before us. It must be everyone's duty to assist in bringing some sort of reason and sanity to this earth plane. Perhaps we can lead many to the Elysian Fields--our Summerland of paradise. That ancient Roman sage Cicero said it best: 'To live with joy and to die with hope is the best thing'. I do prattle on too much, forgive me."

All eyes in the room watched as she sat down. Jack Sewell hated to break into the intensity of the moment.

"Well put, Domina. I want this understood; this will not be a parlor game. All of you have extraordinary powers in clairvoyance and clairaudiance, or at least are in a developmental stage of growth. You are not, as some religious fundamentalists put it, necromancers, or lovers of the dead. We are not Satan worshippers or witches. We are highly developed psychics. But we have to stand guilty on the charge of being in communication with the departed. It is our mission to help others see that death is the entry way to another life. We certainly can't offer the promise of reincarnation since it may not be a truth. Possibly science will catch up with us someday--Let's take our first break."

Donna made a bee-line to Emma and Tom. "Now you know why I didn't have time to call you before I flew to New York. I did it for our safety." Donna saw a faint pout on Emma's face. "Still upset with me, Em?"

Emma smiled, realizing that Donna, even in her wild-hare moments, was the best friend that she could ever hope to have.

"I'm sorry Donna, but sometimes I get into these crazy moods. I like the assurance that you're only a phone call away."

Donna looked directly at Tom. "When you have perfection like Tom around, I think you can survive a few days without me." Donna gently pinched Tom's cheek while speaking to him, "Why can't I have a real man like you?" Tom blushed. "God, you even blush like a virgin, and I certainly know you aren't!"

Emma was waiting for an uninterrupted moment to talk with Madame Redmond. When she saw her chance, she quickly walked across the room.

"My dear, I've heard so much about you."

Emma was startled. She knew what was coming.

"I've been in communication with your maternal grandmother, Reba; a very dear lady. She told me about Valentino and his bracelet. She also sends her love and protection. I hope you don't think I'm prying, but, I've heard about your tragic childhood and your late husband. It seems that some of us suffer more than others. You're stronger than most of us because of these adversities. My dear, you are a survivor, and will survive some rather disconcerting events looming on the near horizon."

"Survive future events? I don't understand."

"The coming episodes in your life, my dear." Domina reached for Emma's hands and held them. Emma was startled at their enormous strength.

"You are gifted, more so than anybody here, except for a special person attending us tonight. You will lead others to the true path in your long life." She looked to Emma's side at the approach of Tom.

VALENTINO'S CURSE

Emma was slightly annoyed at the interruption, wanting to know more about her grandmother and Valentino.

"What a beautiful young man you are, and so gifted. It is very seldom that I get to meet an individual that has brushed shoulders with a Messenger."

Emma watched Tom's befuddled expression.

"Young man, don't be so startled, there is little that goes on in this world that some of us are not aware of."

They were distracted by two of the servers pushing tea carts loaded with coffee and tea pots, along with a goodly selection of French pastries. They left Domina Redmond when Robert Shell came to talk with her.

While Emma was listening to Donna, Emma furtively looked at Madame Redmond and Shell. They were sitting close together holding each other's hands. She had the distinct impression that Domina was in awe of Shell.

Their auras glowed. Several times Redmond's head looked down, then suddenly would bob up with a smile written across her parchment-colored face. Emma thought it strange that Domina Redmond's face had the distinct look of humility written across it.

"Ladies and gentlemen, I have a few words about tomorrow night. Shall we be seated?"

"Tomorrow evening we will follow rigid guidelines for our very special sitting. Our séance will be held as close to the International Psychical Association standards as possible. Donna has graciously given us the use of this room. I don't want to hold the sitting at our church or even at my...Karl's house. I feel many entities are too deeply 'involved' with those surroundings. I will prepare Donna's house in the morning by using the oath of protection, along with the purifying agents of boiling white vinegar and sea salt in every single room. As previously mentioned, Domina Redmond will be our medium. Also remember that we will contact Karl if the conditions are right. Karl should be ready to communicate with us, at least that is what Domina and my dreams have revealed."

Jack's eyes carefully scrutinized every face in the room. "Any questions?" He was the gravest he had ever been.

There were none. They left at eleven o'clock that evening with the promise to gather for the evening séance at seven the following night.

VALENTINO'S CURSE

It was close to midnight when they arrived home. Emma had taught Tom the oath of White Light protection on the way, and after entering the house they separated on cue, with Tom checking the second floor for spirit intrusion and Emma searching the first floor.

Meeting in the master bedroom after their spirit sweep, they crawled into bed and made love, their sleeping potion.

As a prelude to their lovemaking, Tom's mouth feverishly kissed Emma's breasts and stomach. He could feel her desire match his when her hands explored his body. He moaned at her skilled hands, and finding her ready, he made love. Much later, they lay spent and exhausted, wrapped in the safety of each other's arms.

Tom cleared his throat. "I'd like to talk about the séance."

Emma, purred, savoring her contentment, answered.

"Sweetheart, in the morning, let me linger in this moment, this was what I needed, this release. Please, let's not discuss this now." She bear-hugged him while she drifted into a deep, contented sleep.

She entered that special level of sleep she looked forward to. When Emma had been nine years old it had first happened, she had found herself flying in an Out of Body Experience.

She had flown out of an open bedroom window in slow motion. Moments later she had zoomed into the cool night sky.

Emma had felt she could have flown to the face of the blinding harvest moon that night. She had glided and soared high above Chicago, and then over Lake Michigan. She had no recollection of how long her solo flight had lasted, and it took a lot of concentration to fight the pull of permanently leaving her body, but it seemed to her that she could have remained out of her body forever.

Then as quickly as she had left her body, she found herself hovering several feet above her body. In the morning she had a massive nosebleed and a pounding headache that lasted the entire day.

Now she was suspended above her sleeping body safely nestled in Tom's strong arms. A signal in her brain commanded her etheric self to leave the room through the open window. She floated through the open window, the window screen melting away with the contact of her spirit double, her body quickly zooming above the house.

She comet-shot over Chamberlain Observatory Park and the university campus near the house, soaring higher until her spirit body reached the Continental Divide of the Rocky Mountains.

Emma saw Lake Dillon, and the twinkling lights of the towns of Frisco and Silverthorne. She abruptly stopped in mid-air, looped in a stomach tickling somersault, and flashed back to Denver and her home at an incalculable speed. Strangely, she was surprised over not meeting the force or wall of cold air while continuing to fly faster than the interval between a heart beat.

Hovering above the house for several seconds, she quickly descended, joining then merging into the molecules and earth substance of roof and floors, finally ending the voyage by floating above her comatose body then disappearing into it.

Her eyes struggled to open with the sounds of running water coming from the bathroom. She heard Tom lightly humming James Taylor's, 'You've Got A Friend.'

"Come on baby. Time to get up." Tom nuzzled her back. "We're going to take a bath. The jacuzzi will wake both of us up."

She protested, "But I don't want to get up."

Tom easily lifted her from the bed and carried

her into the bathroom where he carefully deposited her into the steaming, white porcelain sunken tub.

Giggles filled with pleasure rolled from her lips as hot water enveloped her body. Her eyes opened, watching Tom hang over into the tub while he adjusted the controls of the six jet openings.

His body fat was non-existent with rock hard muscles tightly packed and planed on his large boned frame. She could feel the heat of desire enter her abdomen. She loved him. He was completely unselfish in giving his love and possessions. If she had asked Tom to give his life for her--which she would never do, she knew he would do so without a minutes hesitation. What was best in their relationship was trust, absolute trust, so there never was a question of surrendering their lives on a whim.

Emma felt a wave of gooseflesh "Ah, oh. The water feels so good!"

Tom slowly slid into the large tub. "Want me to wash your bones?"

"Yes. Um, especially my back."

Emma relaxed while she sat with her back turned to him. She sat in his lap, and it was not long until she could feel his hardness stirring against her. The bubbling, fizzy jets added an extra dimension to the sensuality of the moment.

VALENTINO'S CURSE

They were soon spent after love making, left only with pounding heartbeats and relaxation.

While they briskly rubbed each other down with towels, she said, "I had another Out of Body Experience last night."

Tom said nothing. At first she thought he had not heard her. "I said, I..."

"I heard, I never know what to say. I just don't understand. Never had one myself, or at least I don't think so. Where'd you go?"

"Over the mountains to Lake Dillon and Frisco... and Silverthorne. This makes the third time I've done this. I wonder why. Do you think we could drive up to the mountains Sunday morning and take brunch at the Big Bear Inn? Maybe even stay a night or two. It would be fun to go through some of the antique stores and even take a balloon ride over Vail Valley. You could call in sick."

"No problem." Tom was day dreaming.

"You promise?"

"Yep."

"We must eat something light. I know a salad is not very filling, but you can't eat a heavy meal before any séance."

Tom looked like he was about to pitch a fit. He picked at the cucumber, lettuce and tomatoes, then laid his fork down on the woven place mat looking sharply at Emma.

"This might be my first séance, but damn it, I sure would like to have a black olive and hamburger pizza." She knew it was more than that. He sighed under his breath, he was tense and a little nervous over what might be revealed; he wanted secrets to remain secrets.

His heart thumped with excitement at participating in a real séance, and in only a few hours. He knew there was a reason why he had been chosen to sit with them. Tom shuddered involuntarily, hoping the sitting would not be over what he had been dreaming about the past few days. Very intense. He quickly buried the thoughts of those dreams.

Emma had thrown him far too many unanswered questions which ended up log-jamming his thoughts. Not once, prior to the recent happenings, had she given him an indication that she had really believed or known so much about the paranormal.

Tom battled his mind frequently, searching for the threads that he believed were woven in the mish-mash of the metaphysical tapestry that made up life. He also supposed the denial of death and wholesale pursuit of youth, possessions, and status in the western world was responsible for many people living an empty, purposeless life; this too he believed was hidden in the tapestry of life, waiting discovery by a true seeker.

He had long ago concluded that most people worked hard at deluding themselves into believing they would live forever, thinking they were actually postponing or delaying the inevitable on their terms. Despite his growing bank of metaphysical knowledge, Tom knew he had an abundance of fears left to conquer. In a few hours, he was going to discover more about himself. He knew it, and he was very much afraid.

Chapter 10

Shadows merged with the dim light of the room, making the participants additionally jittery while preparing their emotions for an unwanted séance. The elegant room with the grim-faced sitters was out of a "B" grade movie set from the 1930's. A howling wind further enhanced the other worldliness of the setting by rattling trees that rubbed and stroked the high gables of the roof.

Cathedral-sized candles screwed into elaborate, wrought-iron floor stands were in every corner, their flames insolently flickering and refusing to blow out despite drafts of cool air that seemed to emanate from the very walls.

The candlelight was unable to dispel a sense of melancholy that clung to the museum-like room. Color was barely able to penetrate the eyes of the sitters, further bonding shades of brown and black to an already sepia-splashed room. The thick, white taper sitting in the middle of the round séance table, focused prisms of light onto an antique crystal vase filled with a freshly cut assortment of dead-white, long stemmed Calla lilies.

Emma attempted to capture a sample of the vibrations in the room; nothing evidenced a sense of the malevolent. She thought that Jack's psychic cleansing of the house had worked.

Six people sat around the large table. Jack Sewell sat next to Domina Redmond who was sitting next to Robert Shell. Tom sat next to Shell and Emma sat between Tom and Donna.

Jack spoke. "We will try to be grounded as much as possible during this séance. Once Domina goes into trance, we will remain seated--and very quiet... regardless of what happens. I must impress on you to remain seated at all times! To break our circle of energy and protection could cause great harm. Understood?" Sewell's intensely-focused eyes slowly lingered on every face for registration, eyes to eyes.

Jack paused for a few moments while catching his breath then continued, "I've invited a photographer from the Psychical Research Society to videotape this sitting."

With his remarks, a short, dark-haired young man entered the dimly lit room.

"I would like to introduce Bill Vargas."

Vargas smiled nervously, then commenced setting a video camera on a tripod a few feet to the back of Robert Shell.

Emma met the shining eyes of Shell then feigned looking at the table floral arrangement, but not before she noticed how the candle light threw light on the square planes of his handsome face and his magnetic eyes. The candlelight had penetrated through his copper-brown irises, enough to capture and reflect a golden glow, very much like a cat's eyes caught in the headlights of a car.

Jack interrupted the silence of the room. "A well-managed séance can be a crucial, natural stage in our spiritual progression. Tonight we will be on the borderline between life and the great beyond. Some of you will see more than you thought possible, perhaps even want to. The limitation exists only if you impose a limit. We will start with deep breathing exercises for relaxation then we'll join hands for the energy circle, at which time Domina will invoke the White Light of protection. I hope that through our energy and faith, we will enable a contact with Karl Michael, or his spirit control. Are we ready to begin?"

The only noise in the room came from soft breathing. Emma looked around the table, then again closed her eyes while her thoughts flew to the foot of the 'Door', which she hoped would lead to a complete suspension of her thoughts...then to a perfect Alpha brainwave meditational state.

She had no idea on how long she floated in deep meditation, the next thing she heard was Domina Redmond's soothing voice.

"I bring the eternal forces into our bodies asking for strength, protection and guidance. I further request the White Light of purity and goodness that now surrounds us, to enter us, thus making us one with the eternal astral plane."

Her voice was clear and reassuring, and a little melodramatic, thought Emma. Domina repeated the phrase three times. Emma felt a tingle of energy entering her body, quickly followed by a persistent buzzing in her ears.

She slit her eyes. Domina was surrounded by a six foot high, gauzy aura. The aura seemed to alternate between a brilliant opalescent white, softening to a mottled red-violet color.

The others around the table had mixtures of glowing white and faint yellow auras. Emma glanced at her hands and arms, noticing they were surrounded with an intense yellow color outlined in violet. From the corner of her right eye she marveled at Tom's aura, a translucent, hazy blue.

She felt herself leaving her seated body. She opened her eyes to what looked like a huge space filled with a thick rainbow colored fog. No moisture or coolness clung to the heavy mist, but she had the distinct feeling she was in another world. She was startled at the thought--quickly realizing she was no longer in the room!

Emma stood in a phosphorescent mist. No breeze. No smells. No sounds. He was standing in front of her. Valentino!

"We meet again, cara mia. Welcome to the great, unseen world! Before you ask any questions, let me apologize for my...uh, indiscretion of the other night. It had been so long since I had tasted the earthly pleasure of a beautiful woman...and I could not control myself. You seemed so willing, and I lost control."

Emma was speechless, it did happen!

He continued. "This sitting is a perfect excuse to meet again, for reasons I'll explain later."

At first, Emma noticed he was transparent, then when her mind adjusted to the strange environment, he turned into a solid form. He was melodramatically covered in a shimmering spirit robe with the hood resting across his broad shoulders. His face was pale and handsome. His trade-mark hair was heavily pomaded and slicked back, reflecting the unnatural indirect light.

"I had to get you here to warn you. I'm never allowed to answer questions completely because things that are and will be, must remain a mystery to the earth-plane living, for you who are "alive" must solve these mysteries on your own. The bracelet, mine in my earthly life, is a clue, your clue. Look at it."

Emma held up her right arm to look at the heavy gold bracelet with the elaborate platinum clasp. She gasped at its color. It was a brilliant red, flashing like a warning light on a fire engine.

"I think I should be afraid, but why is it doing this?" Emma could feel it pulsating against her wrist like cold fire.

Valentino drew closer to her. "I'm sorry my love, but it has something to do with your grandmother, and the séance she conducted a short while after my death. I hated being summoned from my initial slumber, and I set things in motion that I should never have done." He looked deeply into her eyes, his liquid chocolate-brown eyes glowing.

"It is very much like a curse or a hex that is

being passed down through your family. However, I can assure you that this mystery will soon come to a head, and a satisfactory conclusion, I trust--but only if you do certain things. You will have to reason these matters out for yourself because that which is written must run its own course."

Emma was distracted by a sharp, piercing noise. Valentino quickly put a finger to his lips. "Shush! Look!"

The phosphorescent mist to her left suddenly split in half like it had been cleaved by a knife.

"Don't say anything," he warned.

She was looking down at the table while suspended over her body. The distortion was strange, similar to a person looking through the wrong end of binoculars. Several apparitions dressed in shimmering silver robes had surrounded the table and were standing to the back of the sitters. Hoods completely covered their heads and faces.

On a cue from another spirit standing directly to the back of Domina Redmond, they joined hands, including Emmas', creating an unbroken circle. The spirit standing to the back of Domina had a long, glistening silver beard that reached to its waist. Emma was awed by the glittering cascade of pulsating white-diamond lights that emanated from his beard.

VALENTINO'S CURSE

Then the next shock occurred. She noticed a white, gooey misty substance oozing from Domina's mouth and nose. While Emma watched in riveted fascination, the wholly implausible happened.

The pearl-white mist oozing from Domina became a gauzy, yet solid looking mass that seemed to grow larger and larger, its substance shaping into a form. In minutes it became a half-sized replica of Karl Michael's face.

Emma found her right hand covering her mouth. She involuntarily gasped. Karl--it, moved its mouth, while mist, like dry ice, steamed from vacant eye holes. Domina commenced talking in a weak, masculine voice even while the ectoplasm flowed from her mouth and nostrils. An odor like freshly brewed tea and a sweet Lilac fragrance filled the room and into the area where Emma floated.

The shrill, piercing noise continued unabated in Emma's ears, blocking completely what Karl's specter was saying. She looked at her now sitting body, then around the table. The sitter's eyes were closed, their hands tightly joined together.

The protective spirits continued to circle and enfold the table and the participants. She noticed the cameraman standing behind the safety of his tripod, Emma suspecting in a state of shock over the enormous blob of ectoplasm clinging to Domina. She knew the video camera would be unable to capture the moment.

The phosphorescent mist abruptly obscured her view, and she heard Valentino's voice breaking into her train of thought.

"Don't ask me, I can't answer for these things. Most things I still do not understand over here."

"Then why am I here?"

"To become aware. Your powers, you have them, but you keep them locked up. For your own protection you must accept these gifts. Your psychic abilities are astounding if you would only use them. As a clue, you must find a way to give me back my bracelet, Pure and simple. For your own safety! Give me back my bracelet!"

Emma continued to be frustrated with his vague answers.

"To show you the power of my world, one day, yours, I know you will want to ask me some questions to satisfy your hunger, a test to see if spirits know everything or anything, but also remember that I can't go into detail...because we're over here doesn't mean that we are all knowing. It's best for your sanity to never know the complete answers. Your time will come eventually. Ask me some questions, and perhaps I will now know some answers." For some reason, he took on the feeling or looks of a defeated earth person, his head even slumped.

Emma volleyed questions like a tennis pro, with Valentino slamming half answers back.

"Was there ever a continent of Atlantis?"

"In men's dreams. But, Perhaps...."

"Reincarnation?"

"Not as it is presently understood on the earth plane."

"Do pets go to the planes when they die?"

"Sometimes, if there was a strong bond of mutual love with their masters. All animals are looked after. Look. My favorite dog is with me." Emma followed his pointing finger. A large Doberman suddenly stood in the mist to his side.

"My beloved Kabar." Valentino gave him a hand command, and the Doberman sat at his feet. "Continue."

"Who really murdered JFK, Bob Kennedy and Marilyn Monroe--and Martin Luther King?"

"Strange, so many are always asking these same questions, but a certain organization, and I might hasten to mention, the men responsible for these deaths, are forever earth-bound entities. Terrible, you should see their punishment! And before you ask, Princess Diana--I am unsure.

"Was Edgar Cayce a genuine, gifted prophet?"

"In many respects, very genuine."

"What about Jesus?"

"There is so much more to his story than any human being could ever understand...the same with the Buddha.

"Will we ever meet God and his Archangels? Do they really exist outside of our minds and our religious institutions?"

"You will have to find these answers for yourself."

"How many dimensions are there, really?"

"Eight, the same number as astral planes, well, perhaps four additional, it just depends on perceptions and your placement."

"Where did that unique, and rather sudden 'spark' of the Mayans, Incas and the other pre-Columbian civilizations come from?"

"What they cared to borrow, came from several sources, primarily from their soul mates, the two lost Etruscan tribes, and the Quartarians."

"Quartarians?"

"Someday their civilization will be found in South America and middle Africa. They are actually a quite fascinating alien civilization."

"Have...are...there interplanetary beings visiting the earth plane now?"

"Presently, no."

"Were the teachings of Jesus and the apostles correct?"

"A very interesting question, Emma. But, mostly correct. As for his apostles, their 'interpretations' became distorted by institutional dogma in order to maintain power or continue the status quo. And before you even ask about the Buddha and the Mohammedans, remember that just because a person like me dies, does not mean we know everything."

"What about Mojo, Channeling, Astrology...?"

"Enough, enough, cara mia. You ask too much! You are wearing me out. Just say that every wistful fool who becomes ensnared by Tarot, black and white magic, crystals, Runes and other such matters, should closely examine their life. Always trust your intuition. Remember that these elusive powers are in all beings, and are without the obstruction of time and space. Use your intuition, then you won't care about the questions you have asked...you will know as much of the truth as you will care to know."

A choking sensation followed by a shudder jolted Emma's physical body sitting at the table.

Valentino drew closer to Emma. His cool breath

smelled like sweet cloves. "It is time for me to go, my strength is weakening. I knew it would be a matter of time until I was found out. Emma, I want you to rejoin your body at once. Hurry! I will meet with you again. Be on your guard, and above all, help protect your lover."

Emma shook loose from the spell-like state. Her heart felt like it was about to explode with the excitement of meeting with Valentino, and the discovery of some of the half-answers he had given her. She fought to regain control while looking around the table. The glazed eyes of the sitters were fixed on the ceiling.

An enormous arm protruded from the ceiling, wiggling and squirming while it slowly lowered itself to the center of the table.

At first the disembodied arm was one-dimensional and transparent, quickly shaping into a flesh colored, three- dimensional hologram. The arm had a distinctly feminine hand, delicate with long, graceful fingers, the fingernails sharp and manicured, painted with a glowing lavender nail polish.

The hand jerked with animation, stabbing and pointing with malice through one finger, almost jabbing the finger into the face of each sitter.

It saved Emma for the final silent accusation,

floating to within several inches of her face. The hand balled into a tight fist, showing considerable agitation by wigwagging inches from her nose. It then abruptly withdrew from her face, where it hung suspended above the center of the table.

The arm then violently slammed its fist into the center of the table, splitting the massive antique library table in half. The noise was deafening, frightening the sitters into breaking their tightly linked hands and the circle of protection. Flowers, water and shards of glass flew across the room, filling the room with a gagging floral fragrance magnifying the sensation of malignant evil.

The arm withdrew into the ceiling suddenly as it had first entered, leaving the room silent and cold as a crypt.

It took several minutes for the sitters to shake off their stunned disbelief. Emma looked up, catching Shell's inquisitive shimmering copper colored eyes. He was the only person sitting at the splintered table who seemed to be in total control of his emotions.

The rattled participants spent an hour retelling what they thought had happened. Tom was silent throughout the discussion, Emma knowing he had been badly shaken more by a personal revelation than the actual events of the séance.

The group was completely disturbed by the threatening arm's appearance. Domina Redmond was at a loss to explain why the malevolent form had materialized, however, the sitters were more excited about the appearance of ectoplasm which had oozed from Domina's head, and an additional discussion ensued about Karl Michael's contact.

Nothing new was really learned from Karl, except the guaranteed promise of a Summerland, and that he was well, happy and working on 'assignments'. All discussion was avoided about the evil force that had entered the room during the séance. Nobody brought up what or who had murdered Karl, afraid that by mentioning the fear they all felt could bring to life further danger. But Jack knew.

Tom, Emma and Shell, remained silent during most of the discussion, each skewered on their own experiences.

Several times during the group's post-mortem, Shell had closely scrutinized Emma, marveling at how she was able to keep the excitement to herself of her visit with Valentino. Numerous times he wished he was not able to see and know so much, it got to be very exasperating when he was not allowed to intervene.

VALENTINO'S CURSE

The sitters were keenly disappointed about Vargas's over-exposed video takes, chalking it up to yet another instance of the secretiveness of the spirit world.

The evening ended with Domina attempting to refocus the group's thoughts on the arm, and the implied threat of violence when it had confronted Emma. When she was met with complete silence, Domina knew it was best to drop the discussion.

Fear again hung like a shroud over the sitters. She thanked everyone for their kindness, enjoined them to continue their spiritual paths, adding that the next time they would meet would possibly be in the paradise of a Summerland.

Chapter 11

Emma and Tom decided to take the promised trip to the mountains, fleeing a brain-frying heat wave in Denver the following Sunday afternoon. The Saturday night séance had been so intense and stressful, that they both felt distance and a change of scenery was needed for a second wind. Agreement was also reached that no conversation about what had happened at the sitting would be shared, or mentioned, until they felt comfortable.

On the first leg of their drive through the mountains, they spotted a deserted inlet on Lake Dillon, surrounded by a thick grove of towering pine trees on two sides and the lake on the remaining side.

Tom spread the Scottish-plaid blanket while Emma arranged the contents of a wicker picnic hamper filled with two bottles of German Rhine wine, a fried chicken, assorted Dutch cheeses, pasta salad, crusty French bread and fruit.

After gorging their fill on the ample spread and consuming two bottles of Rhine wine, they were mellow and tipsy.

"Let's go skinny dipping."

Emma was reluctant. "Somebody might see us."

"Nobody around. Loosen up!" Tom stood up and stripped down to blue boxer shorts. "Come on, the water and the sun will do us good. No mosquitoes either."

Emma impulsively tossed aside any modesty after Tom had waded into the lake naked, all the while pleading with her to join him.

The water was cold and bracing, the surface warm in the high altitude afternoon sun. They splashed, Tom careful not to get Emma's hair wet. After fifteen minutes of bobbing in the water and Tom swimming under water, they were freezing. They ran hand in hand to the blanket.

Tom took her on the blanket. "God, I love sex!" Seeing Emma blanch at his outburst, he quickly apologized. "Sorry. It just feels so great to be here with you."

She could not hold the nagging question back.

"How many women have you had sex with in your life?"

"Honestly babe, I just don't know. Many, but none that could ever be like you. Sorry, am I a macho pig, or what? It doesn't really matter anyway, it's all past history now."

"Have you played around since we've been together?"

Tom looked down at her beautiful face, which was clouded enough to give a deep crease line above the bridge of her small nose.

"None. Honestly. You've been my salvation. I really think I owe it to Travis and you to be faithful."

"Owe it, I don't understand."

"First of all, I love you more than my life. Second, without your understanding--and Travis's, I would've gone down the drain long ago." Tom grew solemn.

"But I thought that an angel, or whatever he was, in that alley in Vegas, was the reason you started flying right."

Tom reached deep in his heart. "It was, but the two of you guided me in so many ways. Hell, let's not get too heavy today. I'll open the last bottle of wine."

They dressed then finished the bottle of wine.

VALENTINO'S CURSE

"Stop here...please."

Tom groaned under his breath. "Don't you ever get tired of looking through antique stores?"

"No. There's the parking lot, see, over there. You know how my prowling through these shops helped to furnish the house, and don't forget those Art Deco lamps I found for your condo."

The only antique store in Silverthorne held an eclectic stock of unusual goods. Along with the bric-a-brack of yesterday's junk, was an enormous collection of hand-painted Tarot cards, esoteric books, wax hex dolls and an unusual jumble of terra-cotta jars containing disgusting smelling herbs and strange things with exotic names. Then she saw it.

Sitting on a oak roll-top desk next to boxes of multi-colored votive candles, was a Plaster of Paris memorial bust of Rudolph Valentino dressed as an Arab sheik. His face and throat were painted in tan flesh tones, while his burnoose and a neck pendant were painted in several faded pastel colors.

Emma picked up the ten inch high plaster bust and held it tightly to her chest.

"Tom, I've got to have it!"

"Okay." He looked into the dark shadows of the room for the clerk. "Hello, anybody here?"

"May I help you?" She was dressed in a floor length black MuMu. The woman had a wrinkled, painted face with heavy make-up that did little to conceal several, purple-colored warts on both cheeks. Tom almost gasped outloud when she stood exposed in the dim light of the room.

"Excuse me. How much is this bust of Valentino?"

The clerk hesitated a few moments, squinted at Emma, then said in a raspy voice, "Not many of these around, but I'll sell it to you for $150." Tom was about to question the excessive price until he saw the pleading look on Emma's face.

"$150? Do you take checks?"

She appraised Tom, then Emma. "Yes, I'll take your check--with two major credit cards for I.D. purposes." Then she quickly added, "It's our policy for outta towners."

When they were getting into the car, Tom looked over at Emma. "You know of course, the bust wasn't really for sale. Em, I have the feeling that its been waiting for you alone. Isn't that strange?"

She looked at Tom. "I was thinking the same thing. She was one weird duck, even had warts. It's best not to make too much of this, because she still charged too much money for something that would probably never sell. Anyway it's good to be out of that shop. Those long finger nails with that lavender nail polish, ugh! and those putrid herbs and other things."

They checked into the Black Raven bed and breakfast in the town of Minturn.

Emma briefly explored the three room suite, then walked to the large balcony that overlooked the chugging river that banked against the side of the inn.

After Tom had placed the luggage on the king sized bed, he joined her on the balcony with two long stemmed glasses filled with champagne.

"Where did you get the champagne?"

"In the ice bucket next to the bed, courtesy of the inn. Gimmie a kiss here or in bed." He looked at her eagerly, hoping she would pick the bed.

Emma giggled. "Sex, is that all I'm good for?" She laughed, and then broke free from his arms; she kissed him lightly on the cheek. "I want to freshen up, and then look the town over."

"Honey, all the Glass men were equipped at birth

to render special services with special equipment. Besides, you know how crabby I can get without a release."

Emma jumped in, "Don't forget what happened to Brad." She was referring to Tom's younger brother who had been shot to death by an enraged husband while in bed with the man's wife. He was also a Satyr, an equipped Glass man. The passing years had pushed the actual horror of Brad's untimely death into the category of family black humor.

Tom feigned a laugh, slightly pained with the memory. "Well, at least the legendary Glass family peckers will continue through Brad's two boys." They both laughed while Tom refilled their glasses.

That evening they walked across the gravel road and dined at the Country Grill cafe. The patrons selected, and then cooked their own steaks over a blazing grill while making a salad with numerous ingredients.

They made love on full and contented stomachs throughout the night and into the early morning. Emma had relented, as tired as she was, and she felt so very strange, sure that something had been set in motion.

VALENTINO'S CURSE

She felt like she had a hangover the next morning. The bright mountain sunshine flooded the bedroom, seeking its way to the rumpled bed where it caressed and massaged its sensuous fingers across her back. Emma reached over to Tom then turned over on her back. She bolted upright, her eyes open wide while she searched the room for Tom.

Tom was on the balcony, Sun reflecting from the perspiration on his naked torso. Faithfully every morning, usually at sunrise, he spent an intense hour doing an exerting, martial routine of Tai Chi movements.

She propped herself on the pillows watching his body move in fluid dance-like cadence. Emma loved watching his heavily muscled body take on a feminine grace while it went through 38 disciplined movements. She had followed his movements, step by step for so long that she could mentally time the seconds of intervals between each position.

Tom walked into the bedroom, sweat now pouring from his hairless chest. "Hi, didn't think you were up." Before she could respond he said, "Want to take a cold shower?"

"No way buddy, I intend to sleep some more."

She heard him shower while she entered a drowsy half-sleep.

The next full day was spent on a hiking trail, and doing tourist things like taking a balloon ride over the magnificent Vail Valley, then renting a Jeep and four-wheeling to a ghost town. They also dined in the most expensive restaurant in Vail.

A considerable amount of time was also spent in each others arms.

The following night they celebrated the last night of their brief vacation. After eating at a secluded French restaurant in the nearby town of Breckenridge, they sat parked on a steep hill that overlooked Lake Dillon. The lights from Frisco and Breckenridge reflected into the still waters of the lake like hot coals.

Tom held Emma tightly in his arms and said, "You know, I think this has been the best mini-vacation I've ever spent. It's even better since I'm with you. I love you so much Em, that I hurt."

She kissed him. "I love you too, Tom. I never was in any doubt about that. It's kind of a shock to me, lightning, thunder and all, but I know you're the only love I'll ever need...or could ever want! She was startled with this revelation, and a dark cloud of betrayal momentarily hovered over her for a few minutes—Travis.

"Do you really mean that?"

Without hesitation she replied, "Yes." She looked at the lights snaking in the lake for several minutes. "This little chunk of time we've stolen has given me the resolve to sort things out. I've already decided to return to teaching at the university this winter, maybe spring...and to accept your marriage proposal, that is, if your offer still stands."

She heard him swallow hard. The silence pounded in her ears while she waited for his reply.

Tom got out of the car and opened her door. "Let's walk to the lake." He could read her thoughts. "It's time to talk."

They walked along the edge of the lake. Tom stooped to pick up a handful of rocks, skipping them across the black water which swallowed the lights from the houses perched on the cliffs above the lake, a silver-black beast gorging itself on rippling lights.

He turned facing her. She was afraid to look into his eyes, instead focusing her gaze onto the lake. She waited for his answer.

"We can't marry now. Ever. It's not fair to you, because I know the hour and the date of my death. Why marry so you can become a widow again? Can't we just continue as lovers? It's much safer for you."

Despite the reservoir of self-control Emma had nourished over the years, which had insulated her from unpleasant moments, especially Travis's death, foster homes and cold academic pursuits of grades and the chase to become an associate professor, an instant splash of warm tears ran down her cheeks. She lost control. The taste of cold salt stuck to her lips and the inside of her mouth.

Incredulous, she muttered, "You know the time and date of your death? How?"

Tom wiped her eyes with a handkerchief from his jacket pocket. "I think I've known for some time, since that Las Vegas alley incident. Remember, it happened just a few years ago. I learned a few more things at the séance. Travis came to me, told me to be prepared. Shit, what do I say Em? What can I say? I don't want to leave this life, not now anyway, but I'm as ready as I'll ever be. And just think, I at least know when, where and even how! I'm not scared, but damn it, there's still so much to do! And as for us...."

She moved closer to Tom, reaching one hand

over to stroke his cool face. "When is...it going to happen?"

"I can't tell you. Let's make the best of the time we have together, okay?"

Her legs grew weak--almost collapsing. She cried. "I love you so much!"

"I know, but not as much as I do you."

While they drove back to the bed and breakfast, she realized she hadn't asked Tom about Travis, what he had looked like and if he had said anything about her or given him a message for her. She felt remorse over losing Travis, but now she might, or would, also lose Tom. Emma fought hard to overcome an attack of depression, knowing the old self-destructive feelings again that Travis had helped her overcome, and would have to be met again. She wondered if she had the strength.

The walls of their suite at the Black Raven Bed and Breakfast shadow-boxed with flickering, incandescent shapes from several candles, which splashed muted tints of color on every object in the room. The lush sensuality of a Russian symphony emanated from a portable CD player adding to their special carnal feast.

The love making was intense with pounding heartbeats relieved by short periods of gasping and swallows of iced champagne. The evening was treated like a final farewell, melancholic passion laced with regrets and ecstatic climaxes. They collapsed in each other's arms—happily spent but yet very melancholic; this moment could never be repeated again.

Chapter 12

Arriving in Denver, Emma purposely lingered in the car while Tom unloaded the backseat and trunk. She felt uneasy and twice attempted to slip into trance to see what was bothering her. She was being blocked by some sort of force emanating from the house; she again felt a wave of dread.

Tom punched the code into the electronic alarm pad on the front door frame, and then turned to wave her into the house. She heard the cursing under his breath while he stood in the entryway.

"Sonafabitch!"

She stood closely to his back while he surveyed the damage.

The entryway was littered with broken glass and the remains of the gilded Louis XVI credenza. The diamond dust mirror which once had hung above the credenza was smashed into slivers.

Tom cautiously walked into the front living room while his rage continued to build. The room was cluttered with slashed oil paintings, upturned chairs and loveseats. Tom was silent while he mentally assessed the damage.

"Go outside while I check the other rooms."

Emma waited for Tom to appear at the front door while she took heavy drags on a succession of cigarettes and nervously paced in the driveway. In less than thirty minutes she saw his grim face. He summoned her into the house with his hands.

Tom seemed to apologize. "Really, it's not as bad as it looks. Really. Three of the Japanese floor vases and a lot of bric-a-brack are beyond repair, I'm afraid. You lost some of the paintings, including the two Dutch landscapes, a few drawers dumped on the floor, and some slashed furniture...weird, silverware tied in knots and thrown all over kitchen, don't ask me how on that one. I can't tell if anything was taken, but I want you to see something in the bedroom."

She followed him upstairs to the master bedroom. The room was a chaotic mess of overturned furniture and broken picture glass, but before she could mentally log the damage, Tom pulled her into the dressing closet.

The eight mirrored closet doors were smeared with something that looked like blood. Tom read her thoughts.

"It isn't blood. It's your lipstick, Look."

Her eyes followed his to the last mirrored door. Scribbled in a florid script were the words: 'SO VERY SORRY TO MISS YOU I WILL KILL YOU LATER KISSES'. Emma threw herself into Tom's arms.

Possessions had always been 'stuff', things to enjoy while she could. Her frequent bouncing from one foster home to the next, had long ago negated any real feeling for things or holding onto objects she was unable to cram into more than one suitcase in a matter of minutes. Her life was another matter. She would not surrender it so readily, spirit threats or not.

They spent the remainder of the day and most of the evening cleaning the house. Emma remained depressed and quiet. Tom was firmly locked into brooding over his impending death. Neither spoke for a long time.

Tom finally broke into the silence. "It doesn't look as badly trashed as I first thought. I wonder if insurance will cover some of the damage?" When Emma did not respond, he continued picking up broken glass in the family room. His eyes were drawn to the copper weathervane on the undamaged coffee table. It was spinning. He looked to see if she had noticed. She was busy cleaning up the contents of the refrigerator from the kitchen floor. In one quick movement he picked up the ice-cold weathervane and dropped it into a trash bag.

Tom growled loudly in anger at the room, spitting out: "Bite me!"

He also could not ignore the smell any longer. Tom reeled from the sweet stench of a cloying fragrance that permeated the family room. Several times he came close to vomiting, but was afraid of upsetting Emma. He felt the sharp coil of fear growing in the pit of his stomach, not afraid for himself, but for Emma.

Tom opened the windows in the family room then sat down on the couch. "Break time. Any beer left? Sit down with me for a few moments...here, next to me."

Three cans of beer had miraculously escaped destruction in the refrigerator. She tossed one can to Tom and opened one for herself. Emma rarely drank beer out of a can, insisting that it tasted like metal. This time she gulped the contents of the can down in three, throat burning gulps.

She looked at Tom. "Do you think they'll come back?"

"I have no idea, but I'd like to know what in the

hell set them off," quickly adding, "What do you think?"

"Tom, don't play with me. You know as well as I do, that these bastards aren't human. I can smell that disgusting perfume, or whatever stink, and what about the un-tripped burglar alarm? It--or them, are looking for something...or us!"

Tom thought for a few minutes. "What can I say? I haven't a clue. I think tomorrow we'd better have Jack purge the house. Maybe he can come up with some sort of protection."

"Sure, just like he did at Donna's house--remember the arm?"

Tom sighed in concurrence. "I'm butt-tired, we can finish cleaning in the morning."

Tom tumbled into bed, immediately slipping into a coma-like sleep.

Emma was about to join him until she saw the smashed picture of her grandmother Reba, which once had sat on the lamp table next to the vanity. She walked over to the broken picture frame which was thrown against the leg of the lamp table. The cardboard backing came off in her hands. Two sheets of time-yellowed paper fluttered to the floor.

She was startled. It was a letter from her grandmother, dead long before Emma had been born.

March 17, 1932

My Darling Emma,

When you at last find this letter, I will have been gone for many years. You are in danger, very serious danger. Several years ago I learned my gifts were 'special'. With this discovery, I realized the many blessings and benefits in using these magical abilities and was able to do wonderful things for many people. These gifts were passed on to my dearest daughter, and she refused to use them. Sadly, it cost her dearly.

She, just like you, turned her back on these powerful abilities, afraid she would be labeled a freak and carrying out the devil's wishes. Unfortunately, if she had only used them, she would not have perished so soon. Knowing better, she still left you an orphan.

I approved of your husband, Travis. I also approve of his brother, Tom. Sorry to say, I will have to welcome them both before you come home.

The slave bracelet given to me by Rudolph Valentino, the very same bracelet you now have, is the key to your renewal and spiritual growth, and safety. Rudy will play a vital role in this personal rebirth, but be very cautious. I can say no more on this matter. I'm so very sorry over what I've done, please forgive me.

The dark spirits who will attempt to destroy your spiritual and physical progress must not succeed, but only as long as you continue to grow spiritually and in knowledge. You will understand this in time if you meet the challenges.

I do love you, and we all wait to greet you when it is becomes your time. Again, don't fear evil, meet it head on. Live a good life!

Your loving grandmother,
Reba

Emma read the time yellowed sheets several times, aghast over the date and the comment about events that were just now unfolding...and Travis and

Tom, even Valentino. Impossible, she thought, but it is.

She almost awakened Tom, deciding instead to let him sleep. She sat on the edge of the bed listening to his soft snoring while she thought. She was emotionally spent over the message from Reba reaching out to her across the years. Emma went into the changing room closet, closed the door and cried hard.

She knew Jack would come to cleanse the house with sea salt and vinegar as soon as he was asked. She was also going to ask him about using the Ouija board. She was deathly afraid of the Ouija, having been told it was much too easy to let a hoard of waiting demon-spirits into the earth plane. Some of the spirit entities could be mischievous, others downright evil in intentions.

However, the Ouija board was a shortcut when used by a skilled person, a device for obtaining immediate answers. She needed the answers before something else happened. Maybe she could even help Tom.

Emma looked at the mantle above the bedroom fireplace where she had placed Valentino's bust after she had entered the carnage of the bedroom. She talked in a soft voice to avoid waking Tom.

VALENTINO'S CURSE

"If it's the bracelet you want, I'll try to get it back to you as soon as I know how. But there's something else, isn't there? There seems to be an omission on your part." She knew the bust would remain mute, but still hoped that he was able to hear her.

She undressed, slipped on a short black satin nightgown, and by habit nervously attempted to smooth out the wrinkles, stalling for time while emptying her mind, preparing for the invocation of the White Light to protect them while they slept.

It came in split seconds when she voiced the words. She became surrounded by a fuzzy white fog, the transparent gossamer cloud growing so quickly it almost smothered her.

Emma continued with the invocation. "We bring the Force of the Cosmos down, into our receiving bodies, asking for strength, protection and guidance."

While she repeated the verse over and over, she watched the bedroom fill with a thick silver-white fog which now clung to the walls and the ceiling, crowding every corner and obliterating every shadow in the room.

Once, the White Light had terrified her, but when she understood her ability to summon and use it...and what it was for, she grew comfortable and secure in its protection.

The light completely absorbed and surrounded the bed. It would stay with them until the morning, and better yet, would drift into and search every room, touch every object, and coat every corner with its protection while driving out the malevolence that stubbornly hung in the air.

She crawled into bed snuggling into Tom's arms. She was on the cutting edge. Tom's pronouncement of his death, knowing the very hour and date of his passing, continued to waffle through her thoughts. Before drifting into sleep, she cringed momentarily in cold terror with the thought of being left alone again. Emma knew she was being selfish, but continuing life without Tom was her final defeat. She wiggled tighter in the protection of Tom's muscular arms.

Jack Sewell watched Emma's fearful eyes then shifted to Tom's cloudy, unblinking blue eyes. "Something is terribly wrong. Domina Redmond said she could feel it the first time she met all of us." "My dear", addressing Emma, "She also said this spirit mass was centered on you. Even Karl Michael said that some grave disturbances were following you, he saw, or felt them at your first séance with us." Emma acknowledged his comments with a non-committal nod. She also knew.

Donna was sitting next to Jack, Emma thought rather close, then watched Donna reach over and tightly clasp his right hand.

Tom glanced at Emma, catching her eye for a split second then winked. It was not so much that Donna was holding Jack's hand, but how she was holding his hand, a slight observation to most, but not from those who knew her.

They were both amused at seeing another conquest. Regardless of the fact that Jack had been labeled gay, Donna had always been rather expert at catching men, actually she was a rather skilled Venus Flytrap. Since Sewell had been openly gay or bisexual, and the lover of the late Karl Michael, the display of affection between the two was still a surprise.

Strangely, Emma remembered several accidental, intimate touches by Jack, but had discounted any further thoughts about the incidents. Tom was a different matter. Jack had been open in his interest of Tom. But Donna? She intuitively knew that Donna and Jack were already sleeping together, so Jack must be a switch hitter.

She also knew that it was none of her business as

to what her best friend was doing, and with whom. Emma only hoped the dalliance would not sap the energy of the gifted Sewell.

A good trance medium--actually any gifted and knowledgeable top drawer conductor in the séance arts, was like a radio receiver. The clearer the mind from earthly interference, the stronger the reception. And sometimes, a very gifted medium could receive like a television set, bringing in a clear, mental picture, sometimes in black and white, and rarely, only with the most skilled mediums, attracting a colored moving hologram for others to see, even with sound--at times. Provided that the medium was clear of the static of churning emotions, drink and drugs, and from the taint of charging money for the use of these psychic gifts, and especially free from Hubris, a pretty good medium could be produced.

Jack Sewell, under the tutelage of the very gifted Karl Michael, had become a "state of the art" medium. Emma's fear was that Donna's emotional needs could be his derailment.

"Is it ready?" Jack looked over at Emma, a now serious expression painted across his face.

Emma led the way to the kitchen where a pan was steaming on the stove, filled with equal amounts of sea salt and white vinegar, some esthetics liked to use only koshered salt.

Jack picked up the pan and walked up the back kitchen stairs to the second level of the house. They could hear him softly speaking. Tom had opened every window in the house and as a precaution, again checked every window on the first floor. Satisfied, he opened the front door.

In twenty minutes Jack returned to the first floor. He totally ignored the quiet group sitting around the kitchen table while he continued walking through every room. His voice was so low that Emma was unable to pick-up one word of the ritual oath meant for driving entities out of a suspected haunting.

In twenty minutes Jack joined them in the kitchen, placing the pan back on the stove.

"Done. I hope this works better than what I did at Donna's house. This time I even cleaned the basement."

Emma looked over at Tom, nodding her head slightly. Tom held the Ouija board. Sewell looked at Emma.

"You really want to use the board?" Before She could reply he continued, "You know how I feel about this, but I'll do it because it was your intuitive request." He sighed.

"Let's sit in the comfortable chairs in the family

room."

They rose from the kitchen table and followed Jack into the adjacent family room.

"Emma, sit across from me."

They sat in the two arm chairs that Tom had moved together.

"I want our knees to eventually touch. Move closer."

Jack placed the board lengthwise on their legs. "I'll bring in Protection, and while we are attempting the communication I want absolute quiet. Please! Emma, are you ready?"

She squirmed in the chair trying to find a comfortable position. Her nerves were shot. Emma nodded to Jack when she was ready.

He closed his eyes while softly voicing the Invocation of Protection. After several minutes he opened his eyes, and then gave a slight movement of his head. They moved closer to each other until their knees touched and both of their fingers were on the moveable message indicator, the Planchette, the three legged plastic pointer.

Emma could feel an instant tingle of energy spread from deep in her solar plexus to her fingertips. Jack's steel-gray eyes bore into her. She knew they had made contact with a discarnate entity.

VALENTINO'S CURSE

"What do you want from Emma Glass?"

Their fingers were ignored as the plastic pointer quickly searched the letters of the alphabet, spelling out, 'H-E-R D-E-A-T-H'.

Beads of sweat appeared on Sewell's forehead. Emma's face went chalk white in color.

"Why do you say these things?"

The pointer quickly slid to the letters. 'S-H-E M-U-S-T P-A-Y F-O-R R-E-B-A-S T-R-A-N-S-G-R-E-S-I-O-N-S'.

Jack looked at Emma. "Who's Reba?"

Her heart beat faster. "My deceased grandmother."

"What happened to get this spirit so pissed?"

"I really don't know. At least I think I don't know." Emma was growing terrified with the spirit's confrontation.

The pointer moved again. 'V-A-L-E-N-T-I-N-O-S O-M-I-S-S-I-O-N W-I-L-L K-I-L-L T-H-E S-L-U-T'.

Her heart nearly flew from her chest. She looked at Tom. A connection with the message on the mirrored closet doors, she remembered! The group blanched at the words.

Jack's voice was quivering. "Can you explain in more detail what Emma Glass has done to upset you? Are you the one who had something to do with Karl

Michael's death and the visits to Emma's house?"

They both held their fingers tightly on the indicator for several very long minutes. Donna and Tom remained quiet, their faces void of expression while waiting for the prolonged letters that might reveal an answer.

The indicator then seemed to take life and haltingly moved to each letter, stringing out the drama.

'I H-A-D E-V-E-R-Y-T-H-I-N-G T-O D-O W-I-T-H K-A-R-L-S D-E-A-T-H A-N-D T-H-E H-O-U-S-E V-I-S-I-T-S T-H-E B-I-T-C-H A-N-D H-E-R M-A-N W-I-L-L D-I-E Y-O-U T-O-O J-A-C-K'.

Jack shuddered in disbelief. He addressed the group. "I told you how much I hate contact through the Ouija board. You're never quite sure who've you let in."

The message indicator moved quickly to the alphabet. 'Y-O-U W-A-N-T-E-D M-E I D-I-D N-O-T W-A-N-T Y-O-U A-S-K M-E N-O Q-U-E-S-T-I-O-N-S I-F Y-O-U W-A-N-T N-O A-N-S-W-E-R-S F-O-O-L'.

Jack composed himself then asked, "I demand to know why you are doing these things."

The pointer immediately moved. 'Y-O-U-R D-E-M-A-N-D-S M-E-A-N N-O-T-H-I-N-G I W-A-N-T B-R-A-C-E-L-E-T'.

Sewell ignored the response, then asked the question. "Who are you?"

'M-Y N-A-M-E M-E-A-N-S N-O-T-H-I-N-G T-O Y-O-U'.

"I command you to tell me your name."

'W-I-N-I-F-R-E-D S-H-A-U-G-H-N-E-S-S-E-Y H-A-P-P-Y N-O-W D-E-A-D M-A-N'.

Jack looked at everyone in the room. He was in doubt that the name given was correct. Sewell again asked, "We are unfamiliar with your name. I again ask, who are you?"

The Ouija board flew violently from their knees, slamming into Sewell's face. His hand reached up to touch the blood flowing from his nose. Donna made a move to wipe the blood from his face with her handkerchief.

"Don't move!" Jack grabbed Donna's wrist tight enough to bring tears to her eyes. His eyes held a sincere apology. "It could still be here!"

Jack held Donna's delicate linen handkerchief against his bleeding nose. "Do you see why I'm so damned afraid of the Ouija? A few years ago I discovered how easy it was for discarnate entities to be drawn through the spirit door by way of the board, even when the protection of the White Light was evoked, and I'll tell you this, they were loathsome!

Concerning tonight's spirit visit, I have no idea of what she, more correctly, it, has to do with Karl or Emma. God, what venom!"

He scrutinized the blood on the handkerchief. Dead silence. They were sure Sewell was soft-peddling the confrontation from the female spirit, and the possible connection with Karl's death.

Sewell's strained voice betrayed his thoughts. "I don't think we should make more of this than it's worth." He looked at the group. "Really...I don't." He felt sick in the pit of his stomach and was close to vomiting.

Emma wondered who Winifred Shaughnessey had once been and why she personally was the target for this demonstration of this spirit hate.

Tom was very concerned with Emma's vulnerability. Two could duke it out with the spirit world, but one person, even with the strongest of powers, becomes a toss-up. He sighed in resignation, knowing that his final days possibly had been marked, checked and underlined.

His life was nearing closure. Once he had enjoyed playing the role of a suicidal moth lustfully teasing a candle flame. In that death-wish period he could have cared less about whether he had lived or died, but when he had been given a horrific vision from a angel messenger in a sleazy alley, he grabbed at the life-ring.

Tom felt 'clean' and ready, to face death with bravado and aplomb, armed with his typically bizarre sense of humor, knowing he had the balls to spit in the face of spectral injustice, even while it squeezed and sucked the last of his life juices.

The winged messenger, Tom was not actually sure now if it was winged because of the darkness of the alley, had warned Tom about the immediate changes needed to thwart the damnation of his eternal soul. He had followed the warning within a single heartbeat.

During his first séance, the spirit of Travis had revealed to Tom the hour of his death, the exact day, month, year and hour, and how and where it would happen--and the terrible pain of the last moments of his transition. Tom had cried like a baby in the bathroom after the séance while the faucets were jetting full force, muffling his sobs.

Jack stood up. "Join hands, and please don't break your grip. I mean it. Hold tight! We've got to send it back."

His baritone voice dropped an octave when he spoke the Oath of Protection. After the invocation had been uttered three times, they were immediately surrounded by a bitter, ice-cold blast of wind that flash-froze the fear racing up and down their backs. The room temperature plummeted from 70 degrees to freezing temperatures in seconds.

Sewell continued with the incantation. "I send you back to the protection of your own kind. I send you back to the peace of your world. Leave us in peace. Leave us to our kind, the living. Go with the love and blessings of the eternal universe. Depart from us...now!"

The room shuddered. They held each other's hands in a vise grip while the house groaned in movement. They could hear the rattle of utensils and the clattering of plates in the kitchen cupboards. Several corks exploded from the bottles in the kitchen wine rack. A picture in the hall was slammed to the floor, scattering glass over the oak floor. Booming thuds were heard in the room above, along with cat-like shrieks from the basement.

The room exploded in blinding light while flashes of gray-green light burst from the ceiling, shooting a thick, gauzy-cold mist into the room.

Silvered forms emerged from the cloudy, goo-like ether. Four naked male spirits appeared a few feet from the group, while a distinctly female entity lingered in the clouded ether of the background.

VALENTINO'S CURSE

The male faces were grotesque and ugly in the diffused light that almost masked them. Their distorted faces held empty eye sockets with mouths twisted in snarls of hate. They exuded the combined stench of rot and mildew.

"Go back! We meant no harm! I call down the Protection of the White Light. I command you to leave us!"

A searing white light came from nowhere, immediately enveloping the ether. The male demon-spirits contorted in anguish, twisting and wriggling like berserk dancers in a modern dance interpretation.

Emma observed the female wraith standing motionless in the background shadows. She was whip-slender with boyish hips and rather strangely, was endowed with large breasts. Her hair was bobbed and colorless in the mist. Her face was as featureless as an egg.

Emma's eyes were riveted to the entity's hands that waved at her tauntingly. Delicate fingers were capped by long, well-manicured, lavender-painted nails. Emma had seen the hands and the nails before on the disembodied arm at the last séance, and on the wretch of a store clerk in the mountains where she had purchased the bust of Valentino.

The room was filled with static electrical discharges. Lilliputian lightning bolts flashed then zapped around their heads.

In mini-seconds the entities were gone, but not before Emma saw Robert Shell and Valentino standing in the shadows of the south corner of the room, near the kitchen French doors.

Valentino was smiling at her, Shell stood next to him, his Herculean mass overpowering the diminutive Valentino. His eyes were closed.

She looked at Tom to see if he had seen them, then looked back at Shell and Valentino. They were gone.

Shell! How did he get into the house so suddenly, then disappear so quickly? Emma mumbled under her breath, "Well, well. Detective Robert Shell continues to surprise", she thought.

The small group spent the remainder of the evening in discussing the Ouija board and the spirit display of power. Nothing concrete was arrived at. Strangely, Donna remained quiet, thoroughly focused on Sewell's explanation of the evening's events. It had been a terrifying evening of confrontation, filled with drama and fear, maybe even touching on their very survival, and yet the participants had remained distanced from displaying any surface emotion.

If anyone had had any remaining doubts about the supernatural world, up to that time and about the reality of a spirit world, and that there were malevolent entities, then all doubts were completely and utterly dispelled. None of them would ever be the same again, ever. And for some unexplained reason, the previous run in with the detached arm and fist at the first séance had been totally ignored.

Emma sleep walked through pots of weak coffee while Donna grudgingly threw together a huge mound of roast beef sandwiches. Strangely, everybody was hungry. The only thing that belied Donna's calm exterior was when she had nearly cut herself several times while slicing meat.

"Em, did you see the wangs on those creepy guys? And those bodies! It still takes my breath away! Ugh, the faces though!"

"Good God, Donna! Just remember what could've happened tonight, courtesy of those bodies--we saw them as they once were. I thought those were some of the most horrible excuses for faces I've ever seen!" Emma continued after nervously swallowing, "When are you going to tell me about Jack?"

"I was planning to, but it happened so sudden.

You haven't been home anyway. How about meeting me at the Brown Palace for afternoon tea? Yes, that sounds good, next Thursday at two?"

They rejoined Tom and Sewell with the refreshments.

"Jack, why wasn't Robert Shell invited tonight?" Emma watched his expression carefully.

"He's on duty, investigating a murder, something like that. Hard working guy, really gifted my sources tell me, but works rotten hours. No social life to speak of, what an asset he would be to the church if he ever had the time. I suspect he uses his gifts in his line of work, though. About two weeks ago I read in the Post that he was on a roll in solving six previously closed murder cases. Really gifted. One handsome hunk of a man, can't understand why he hasn't been hauled to the altar yet."

Emma saw a faint glimmer of excitement in Jack's eyes while he talked about Shell, Emma wondering if Donna had read his obvious interest.

After they were alone, Emma and Tom made love, greatly relieved that the visitors from the invisible world were finally vanquished from the house.

They made one error in this assumption.

VALENTINO'S CURSE

Valentino excitedly watched their lovemaking. He had abstained faithfully from participating in earthly pleasures ever since his bed visit to Emma. He now thoroughly enjoyed his role as a spirit voyeur, but sighed in self-pity. Being dead did have some drawbacks.

Chapter 13

Emma stood in the sunken bathtub while Tom repeatedly squeezed and rubbed a large natural sponge over her back. She always looked forward to having Tom bathe her and wash her hair, especially when he massaged her neck and back.

She sat nude at the vanity table while Tom methodically brushed her wet hair with an antique silver brush. Her languid eyes were closed in pleasure with each gentle stroke while her thoughts meandered over the past events of the last few weeks.

She bent forward to rummage through the jewelry box intending to look for Valentino's slave Bracelet, but then decided to relax and enjoy the pleasure of Tom's brushing. She hummed while one hand brushed and the other smoothed her damp hair. Occasionally Tom's hands would gently cup her breasts while he bent down to kiss her neck and ears.

He thought of his approaching death, his termination, the final moments of a brief visit in life.

VALENTINO'S CURSE

Tom watched himself in the mirror, thinking about the exquisite pleasures of life and savoring the little things like brushing Emma's beautiful hair.

Tom was very pleased with how well he had reinvented his life. He was rich, athletic, and well liked. He had even developed a personal code of morality, and for once he had learned to love honestly, to give his heart and not expect payment. He was quick witted, but never burdened himself with "weighty facts". Bulldozing his way through social and business competition with his ruthless appeal and charm, most people he encountered were delighted to accept his simplification of problems and situations. If he came close to losing, he had used his body to gain advantage. Male or female, it had not bothered his weak non-existent conscious. But, that was "then."

He jumped into many short lived careers. Almost a professional college student at one time and very much afraid of making a living without the support of the Glass money. A quick stint as an athletic director on a cruise line turned into boredom with easy conquests. He dabbled briefly as a copy writer at an advertising agency which led him into modeling, and for two years he was one of the higher paid male models in the world. He had several bit parts in

Hollywood, making pretty good money as a porno "star" as he started his downward slide.

Despite heavy drinking and a dalliance with heavy drugs, he always managed to exercise and force himself to eat two square meals a day. He was a fanatic on vitamin usage, even while taking drugs, believing that fistfuls of vitamins would negate the effects of substance abuse.

For a while the delusion worked until he discovered heroin. Then he seemed to implode. His growing habit was supported by stealing and prostitution while he drifted aimlessly from coast to coast. He had almost died in the sewage of an alley, rescued from suicide by the warning etched in the reflection of the golden-eyes of the dark angel Messenger.

Tom had reached the conclusion four years ago that life was good. He had totally revamped his self esteem and rebuilt his body, and with an infusion of Travis's money, became an "instant" success as one of America's exercise kings via cable television.

The international computer and software company that had hired him to establish an exercise program for its stressed-out executives, was so delighted with the results that it underwrote his videos, taking only a minor percentage of the production costs.

Tom had discovered long ago that vitamin

takers, runners and neurotic exercisers thought they could cancel time and block diseases, thinking that the worship of health, natural foods and a certain self fanaticism for money making, would delay and perhaps scare away the monster that hunted the poor and the sick.

Tom was now a product of American Mega, Inc. A winner, a multi-millionaire, an up-beat advisor to a corporate obsession with youth and money; an anointed knight who would assist them in the banishment of the evil beast of age, fat and wrinkles, arming them in this struggle with low fat Yogurt and exercise.

Emma represented everything in a woman he had ever wanted. A slightly older woman who was stunningly beautiful, intelligent, aggressive, sweet-natured and not afraid of being sexual; a hint of a mother that every young man looked for in a woman.

They were an excellent match. Tom had always known that with time, they would have married. The only reason he hadn't made moves on Emma long ago was because of his beloved brother. Travis was the perfect big-brother that every sibling dreamed of having. Tom had deeply loved his brother without reservation, thus, he had kept his distance from Emma while Travis had been alive.

The love affair with his new life had now turned upside down with the revelation of his impending death. Tom was accepting, this was just the way things were. He knew he had no power to change destiny. At least they had loved, and loved well. Perhaps they would meet again on the other side, and maybe even special physical and emotional love needs were granted over there. Anything and everything was possible in this cosmos, he knew.

Yes, he believe strongly in the anything was possible in the saga of a human being! Tom had no regrets, well, almost none. If only that damned slave bracelet of Rudolph Valentinos' had stayed out of the picture, out of their lives; but karma was karma. Piss on it! There was no outside chance of his ever being able to change this outcome.

He sighed deeply with regrets. Tomorrow was the last day of his life! Tom held back an instant rush of depression. Emma turned and looked up at him because he had stopped brushing her hair.

"I love you so much." She held her tears back.

They kissed, and he bent down and picked her up in his arms, carrying her to the bed.

Valentino stood at the foot of the bed watching them make love. He actually cried in genuine remorse for the parting lovers. He had noticed on several occasions that his Italian temperament and emotion had remained with him, even through his transition into death.

Tom sat on the eleventh floor balcony of his condominium, looking down at a sun-washed Washington Park. The view always took his breath away. The forest of Broccoli treetops in variegated green shades surrounded and framed two small, sky blue lakes and an enormous flower garden. The balcony gave an eagle eye's perspective of silently gliding above a miniature forest.

He drained the last of the chilled champagne from a long-stemmed Baccarat fluted glass, nervously sitting the delicate glass down on a black marble table that seemed to cling to the illusion of a floating balcony. Tom remained restless wanting to slow the inevitability of the last day of his life.

He had kept the 2,400 square foot condominium unit, insuring a place to live if Emma had ever thrown him out of her house. He hoped that Emma would not sell the condo because it was an excellent investment, now worth three times what he had paid for it two years ago.

Mentally inventorying the starkly decorated

rooms, he marveled at how his taste had changed recently. Every piece and stick of ultra-modern furniture was veneered in black and white. The walls were stark white, the Swedish hand-woven, wool carpets were black with off-white borders. The extensive collection of simple, Zen-gram paintings and cold-cast bronzes by his favorite Spanish sculptor, Deo de Blanco, were in every room. They had cost a small king's ransom then and were worth an even bigger fortune now, especially since the artist had died.

The rooms were antiseptic-clean, coldly sophisticated and a status seeker's delight. He recently had changed 180 degrees in taste from a preference in Pueblo Indian pottery mixed with rough-hewn south-western furniture and colorful Navajo rugs. A sudden whack of reality refocused Tom's thoughts. He sat down at the massive black acrylic desk and began to write on personalized, dove-gray note paper. He thanked Marisa Laprella, his housekeeper, for looking after him like a mother. He slipped a cashier's check for $50,000 into the envelope tucking it in the corner of the silver-tooled leather ink blotter.

A note was quickly penned to Tony McGille, his training assistant-partner, giving him complete rights to Tom's business except for half of the residuals from the exercise videos, which were given to Emma for distribution to several non-profit animal and homeless foundations.

All monies and mixed investment portfolios were squirreled away in several European and Caribbean bank accounts, the value exceeding well over six million dollars.

Tom spent two hours writing brief notes to his best friends. He left all of his real estate holdings to Emma to dispose with as she saw fit. When he thought about his art, residuals, three recent video sales, real estate and investment portfolios, his total worth was probably approaching a tidy sum of eight million dollars--not bad for a last minute career change.

His hand written will was a hurried duplicate of the official will he had executed with his fishing buddy and attorney, Bill Walgrun. Tom wanted to insure that Emma would not receive any surprises from the lawyer and the IRS.

Tom rose from the desk, stretched, and walked out to the balcony where he drained the last of the champagne. He refilled the glass nervously with shaking hands, splashing most of the bottle's contents onto the balcony carpet, almost dropping the bottle. Ordinarily he would have cursed then sprinted for the kitchen, picking up a dish towel to quickly wipe up every drop of a spill.

Not this time. The additional motion would be pointless...for a dead man. A living flesh and blood mortal, waiting for the dead and discarnate to take him away in a few short hours. His eyes teared with another realization: This was actually it. No reprieve, nothing, at least in this life.

He felt a growing anger rise over why he had been singled out to punish Emma's family line. A curse that involved Emma then himself. Guilt by association. He thought of the stupidity of a universe that allowed the dead to punish the living. Tom didn't blame Emma at all for his misfortune because he loved her heart and soul. Punished for love!

Favorite quotes ran through his mind: 'This chronicle of smoke, this strange and bitter miracle of life'. 'If a man dies, shall he live again?' Other phrases spun through his mind, jumbled and nonsensical.

Fear again turned to anger. He would at least be leaving a world of hate, greed and misfortune; no more obsessions with time and racing to fill days. But he would also be leaving the pleasures of love, sex, challenges, and many other good things he had come to enjoy, things to flourish and nourish his soul with.

VALENTINO'S CURSE

Now he was close to scratching and clawing. Honestly, he did not want to leave his life yet, and he searched deep in himself for the dignity and resolve to exit with class.

Tom eventually settled down and finished another bottle of champagne while he skimmed through several picture albums. His thoughts again turned to Emma while his head buzzed from alcohol and fear.

Emma, he thought. How hard it had been to see her this morning, knowing that it was the last time he would ever see her in this life. He had made the excuse that he had to go to the office for a quick appointment. It had been hard to lie because she was so adroit at reading him. He was going to miss her terribly.

At five o'clock he felt the temperature drop suddenly when a brisk coolness flooded the room. He shuddered involuntarily, then became alert. He looked at his watch. It was time.

The first thing he saw was a cloudy, gaseous-like puff of black smoke. In seconds it quickly materialized into a menacing fog that filled the entire living room and kitchen area.

Several dark transparent apparitions emerged from the cloudy mass, turning into monk-shrouded black shapes, opaque yet somehow solid, and all floating towards him. One figure stood in front of the other malevolents.

At last! He was sure what the whole damn thing was about! With this realization the wraith struck him solidly in the chest, crushing his chest cavity. The intense pain was negated by sharp-nailed fingers ripping his throat open. Tom could feel his brain burst from the incredible pressure of pain.

He was dead before his body was carried to the edge of the balcony and thrown down eleven stories to the parking lot like a freshly slaughtered side of beef on a meat packing floor, splattering and fouling several parked cars on impact, car alarms announcing his slaughter. His soul had already departed at the moment of his mortal death. Tom slept, waiting for his spirit guide to appear and lead him through his next transition.

At that exact moment, Emma was raising an English bone china tea cup to her lips. She involuntarily dropped the tea cup and saucer to the floor.

"My god, Emma, are you okay?" Donna grabbed her hand, instantly feeling the sensation of death lick its way up and down her back at Emma's cold touch. Donna had to go into her inner self to block the revulsion and fear that almost made her swoon. She yelled to the women standing around them, "Call 911, hurry!"

Several women at the Chancellor's tea could also feel the vibrations of death shooting from Emma's prone body. Two fainted from the thoughts they received.

Emma tore through her bottomless handbag looking for a stray cigarette. She silently cursed, disgusted with her lack of will power breaking yet another heavenly vow to quit smoking.

"Dammit...Donna, can I have one?"

"Sweetie, here!" Donna offered a package of cigarettes and a gold lighter. "Em, are you okay, you're so pale."

"I very much feel like shit, thank you!" She gave a weak, apologetic grin while lighting a cigarette with trembling hands, deeply inhaling then quickly exhaling in split seconds. She looked at the clusters of surrounding tables in the Brown Palace hotel's atrium at the entrance to the non-smoking section.

They were detached from the busy hive of tea-takers attempting to be seen in the right place with the right people; the grating, look-at-me laughter was drowned out by the clattering of dishes and eating utensils, and a third-rate string ensemble. A tall, willowy server caught Donna's eye and decorously floated to their table. He simped, "Ladies, may I offer tea and sandwiches? Pastries?"

Donna responded. "Yes please, a pot of Earl Grey, uh, also watercress and cucumber sandwiches. Another tea strainer, this has something strange looking on it."

The young waiter stared at Emma while his mouth hung open, thoroughly fascinated by the powerful vibrations emitting from her eyes. Catching Donna's glare, he hurriedly turned and walked away.

"Good grief, you'd think he had just seen your tits!" Donna lit a cigarette. "Honey, I'm still devastated over Tom. Are you sure we can smoke here? I'll never be able to really comfort you, the only sure thing I can offer you is the thought that he has gone on to another plane of cosmic development, which is really what you don't want to hear right now. I've always felt that the real grief a person has to go through is frequently overlooked by everyone until it visits them. Remember the family deaths I went through? Well, you will endure and actually survive! My rotten little heart broke several times. Remember when I drank too much, well, I survived, maybe as a world class bitch, but I endured. You will too, Em. I swear it."

"At this point, Donna, I don't know how I'm going to survive without him. He's physically dead, and the promise of eternity doesn't make me feel any better, I mean, on to another life is all well and good, but I'm still alone. I'm going to miss him so much. Tom loved me and I loved him." Emma wiped her eyes with a table napkin.

"Tell me about your life with him, it's the best way to deal with pain. Now...come on." Donna held Emma's hands tightly.

The words poured out of Emma while Donna listened. It took over an hour. When Emma became completely drained, they sat in catatonic silence. Donna's eyes glistened with tears while she mentally replayed what Emma had said.

"Donna, I feel so empty...I don't know what to do."

"Em, it's done. He's gone. You have a right to mourn. You're right about earth-bound demons and their involvement in this, but I'll tell you what Jack thinks. These ghouls have been waiting in the shadows all along, confusing us with false clues while throwing us off track. They've had a purpose all along. Jack thinks this evil force, which is growing stronger every day, is after all of us, he's felt the intensity of their vibrations."

"Donna, I swear, no matter what it takes, I'll pay them back, if not here, then over there, but I will!" With that declaration Emma became resigned with the loss of Tom and for the first time in her life, was really filled with the elixir of vengeance.

They finished the second pot of tea in the gilded Brown Palace Hotel's grand atrium, the brass chandeliers, antique Persian carpets and French furnishings lending an elegant and indifferent stage setting to their tragedy. No doubt these same hotel walls had been party to many stories of heartbreak in its hundred years of existence, but it was also doubtful that these walls had ever overheard a more bizarre conversation.

Chapter 14

Tom's memorial service was held a week after his death at Saint Luke's Methodist Cathedral in a seedy part of downtown Denver. Because of the anticipated large number of mourners, Tom's mother, who had been married in the cathedral, decided it was the only suitable place to properly recognize the final bow of an errant, but aristocratic son who had refused to take his rightful place in Denver society and her life. Every hand-carved, Victorian pew was tightly packed with Tom's friends, past lovers and business associates. Shirt-tail relatives that Emma had never met, crammed the three family pews to the right side of the altar.

Emma had planned a simple Spiritualist service, but had been overridden by the minister and Tom's mother, a devout Methodist, who had flown in from Florida at the last minute, leaving the heart-breaking pain of details to Emma. Emma had forgotten why Travis and Tom never visited or extended an invitation to their mother. Now she again remembered why.

Corrina Glass was blatantly an obnoxious bitch and proud of her reputation as such. Age and wealth had turned her into an overbearing dragon lady. Travis had been thoroughly convinced that she had driven his father into a fatal heart attack by her non-stop, vicious nagging. Tom never talked about his mother, afraid the very mention of her name would bring her in on the next wind.

In an early-getting-to-know-you, previous meeting, Emma had found her to be witty and saccharine sweet, but soon discovered that Corrina's take-charge demands with Emma and her sons, could quickly become sharp-tongued and vicious if her wishes were denied. Corrina could bring her prey to tears before they realized they had been gutted.

Luckily for Emma, Corrina was staying with friends buried deep in a gated suburb, and since she did not drive, she issued her decrees over the telephone, such as nixing Emma's plans for the Spiritualist memorial service.

Emma was also cajoled into hosting one luncheon and two sit down dinners for Corrina and her eight friends. Emma had had the foresight to cater the meals, but asserted herself by refusing to change the menus, despite Corrina's continued requests for several last minute changes to accommodate her friend's special diets.

Corrina Glass had never approved of Travis's marriage to Emma. "No family," she sniffed several times. But Travis showed gumption for the very first time and stood up to his mother. Years earlier he would have caved in to her wishes, but when Travis married, he was eligible to tap into a vast trust fund set up by his father; it gave him complete freedom from his mother's dictates.

Tom was a different matter. Corrina Glass knew Emma and Tom were living together, but could have cared less--as long as her friends were unaware of the arrangement. By her unshakable standards Tom was a moral degenerate, the worst of her three sons, and a lay-about who happened to fall into a windfall of money from silly exercise videos and several best selling health and nutrition books.

Regardless of the tragic deaths of her sons, she held little remorse or sorrow, feeling that she was completely blameless and detached from their lack of following her example and guidance to life and deportment, clear and simple. It is doubtful that she shed many, if any, tears.

And since Emma was an older woman, and a

'used' one at that, one who could never provide her with grandchildren--thereby leaving her nothing to discuss at club luncheons, she wanted to get through this final 'affair' and sever all connections with her widowed daughter-in-law.

Corrina knew that a few misguided people considered her to be heartless, she quickly countered with how would they have handled the tragic deaths of three sons--their very own flesh and blood, and of course, a dear husband's passing thrown in.

Emma clearly knew that as soon as the service was over, she would never see or hear from Corrina again, ever, ever, ever again!

The traditional funeral service was formal, elegant and depressing, the profuse and lavish flower arrangements throughout the cathedral, and a string ensemble mixed with an upbeat classical male quartet added the only relief from total morbidity. The two ministers appeared gleeful in prolonging the length of the service, were miffed with Emma, reinforced by faux angst from Corrina.

Emma had somehow convinced Corrina to let the funeral director plan the non-religious part of the service. Corrina had wanted an open casket ceremony, Corrina and the ministers not knowing what Tom's mortal remains looked like, the casket was sealed and locked just before the service commenced, and before the ministers and Corrina had a chance to raise any objections.

At the foot of the six stepped altar was a 56 inch television set connected to four monitors spaced throughout the cathedral in order for participants to observe the service. Instead of a traditional eulogy, a special video was shown with scenes of mountain flowers swaying in the wind. Waterfalls, lakes and streams, grassy fields with grazing deer, all synchronized with movements from several of Tom's favorite works by Vivaldi and Bach.

Following the completion of the first two Bach cantatas, highlights from Tom's life appeared on the screen, a collage of favorite slides and videos that Emma had lovingly selected from Tom's personal collection.

Donna tightly squeezed Emma's hands in reassurance when Emma began to cry. Donna had been impressed with how well Emma had held up through the lengthy memorial service.

Emma nudged Donna. She was looking in the direction of the altar. Donna followed her eyes, at first not ascertaining what Emma was staring at. Then

Donna also saw Tom. His shade was utterly lifelike. He was sitting on the top step of the altar scratching his white blond hair. His face was chalk-white in pallor and he was dressed in a long white robe that matched the paleness of his hands and face. He fumbled with the hood of the spirit robe, pulling it over his head several times, finally letting it drop across his shoulders.

Tom looked up, sensing their stares. He looked at Emma and Donna for several minutes then broke into a wide smile.

Dark circles outlined his eyes, and these circles, instead of adding a death-like grimace to his still handsome face, strangely emphasized his opaque blue eyes.

He stood up and waved while he glided toward them. He stopped, then turning his face to the altar, he smiled. Their eyes followed his.

Travis stood next to the Reverend Davis who was quoting passages from the Bible. Emma held her breath while she squeezed Donna's hand. Travis's eyes were riveted to hers'. The look was of love. Her heart was pounding so hard she felt close to fainting.

The only men in her life were together, brothers joined in eternity. She was suddenly released from the cloud of depression, feeling light-headed with a rush of giddiness coursing through her body. She bit her lip to stop from laughing for joy.

They were okay! Emma now had the final proof. No longer a nut case dealing in mumbo-jumbo and wishful thinking, she was observing the bottom-line truths of life after death.

She had viewed several sides of death at the séances and had tingled with fear in the haunting of her house, now she also saw the side that was more relevant to her. The brothers were together again, looking well and happy. Tom was obviously perplexed over his recent transition, but Travis was proof that a good transition could occur.

Tom glided to where Donna and Emma were sitting. When he was in front of Emma he bent down and kissed her on the forehead. He patted Donna on the hand. Both women felt an ice-cold chill. They also smelled the fragrance of Tom's favorite cologne, Exeter.

Travis joined them, also kissing Emma on the forehead. Corrina, sitting next to Emma, shivered, looked over at Emma, squirmed several times, then resumed listening to the reverend.

Emma's heart still raced with excitement, so much so, that she was almost unable to suppress the laughter that welled in her throat. Life after death! It is true! She looked up at both spirits, and was about to speak. Travis held a finger to his lips for her silence. Tom also appeared to be talking to her, but his voice was either blocked or too weak to be heard.

In a split second, the brothers had swooshed to the center of the dias, physically passing through the body of Reverend Davis who continued speaking from the podium. They paused to look at the audience, smiled as Travis pulled Tom to his side. They waved farewell, disappearing in a cloud of white fog.

The Reverend droned on, "Oh death, where is thy sting? Oh grave, where is thy victory? Death, what is thy message?"

Emma was growing dizzy with excitement. She wanted desperately to tell somebody about this spirit visit. For some reason she remembered an inane quote from the Chinese philosopher, Chuangtzu: 'You cannot reason or talk with a summer insect about winter ice'.

And she mentally thought, "You also cannot talk to a person about the meaning of death and the continuance of life if there is no frame of reference, or belief." But, she had her proof.

VALENTINO'S CURSE

The funeral service reception was held at Emma's house. Every room on the first floor groaned with the weight of people dressed in black or navy blue. True to Yuppie funeral cliches, the majority of women were armed with a single strand of pearls.

Conversations reached the buzzing level of a bee hive ready to swarm when more wine was drunk. The clang of glasses and ting of silverware against plates and coffee cups magnified the noise in the hive.

Emma was the focus of unwanted attention, which dragged her into the role of reluctant hostess. Several times Donna came to her rescue when she had been cornered by overly aggressive people whom she barely knew; she didn't want to talk about death anymore. They hinted at wanting to know the grisly details of Tom's death or to share their opinions of what had probably happened. Two men had even openly made an attempt at snaring the grieving 'widow'.

Donna's appearance had ended a potentially ugly scene when Emma had come close to throwing a cup of coffee into the face of Tom's boss who had offered more than a condolence.

Emma had gone to the bedroom to freshen up, regain control of her composure and mainly to think about how her life would proceed without Tom. She sat at the vanity to apply a light touch of makeup when she felt his presence entering the room.

"I'm sorry to bother you, but you were surrounded by too many people. Strange how people are at their worst in funerals, weddings and holiday dinners."

Robert Shell stood in the doorway of the master bedroom dressed in an expensive, perfectly tailored Armani suit that high-lighted his pale, handsome face. His amber-colored eyes were intensely penetrating, his aura a blinding gold.

Emma, mildly startled by his sudden appearance, continued dusting her high cheek bones lightly with a sable hair brush. She looked at the vanity mirror with a quick glance, noting the patch-up work did little to banish her somber eyes and tightly-drawn face. She was washed in a heavy fatigue that makeup could do little to hide.

He held a long-stemmed wine glass half filled with red wine. "I don't make it a habit to enter a lady's bed chamber without an invitation, but I was wondering how you were holding up...actually what I could do for you."

"Do for me? Robert, I have no idea of what anyone could do at this point. I lost somebody I took for granted. I doubt I'll ever have a chance to love like this again. Oh, I'm sorry, just feeling out of sorts... please excuse my woe is me feeling." Emma knew she was rambling and immediately stopped.

"Yes, you and Tom had something very special. Don't apologize, it's only natural." His voice softened into a whisper. "I saw them at the church you know--Tom and Travis. I also know you and Donna saw them. Doesn't that give you some sort of comfort? Few people are blessed with these kinds of visits."

Emma slowly turned from the vanity and looked up at him. "You confuse me. Who are you--really?"

He looked deeply into her troubled sea green eyes. "You know who I am—I'm your guardian. You saw me with Valentino, suspected something at the garden party, and you know that I'm not what I've spent a lot of time fabricating. I'm here. Simply put, to protect you from them, kind of a special bodyguard from the Other Side."

Emma was close to fainting with this declaration. Another surprise in a long series of surprises. She remained speechless.

Robert continued. "I'm not real as you know real...and I'm not dead, ugh, how I loath that word, as you know dead. I'm here to guard you until you work out this deadly puzzle that has gotten way out of hand."

She did not question or mull his words over. She knew he spoke the truth, an unusual truth, granted. It also frightened her by her quick acceptance.

"What should I do?"

"Let me move in with you. You'll be much safer. I don't have sex and eat only when fed...just like a well behaved house pet. I'll look after you until this mess is concluded."

"When do you move in, if I let you, what kind of protection?"

He ignored her question. "It should be tonight, as soon as everyone leaves. It might not look good, but you need me."

Later that day after the house was empty, Shell said, "I admire your complete trust, just on what I told you."

Emma lifted the steaming coffee cup to her lips, "Do I really have a choice?"

After sharing a light meal from the remnants of the reception food, She showed him to the guest bedroom next to the master bedroom. He carried two large overstuffed, navy blue nylon athletic bags, which he dropped in the middle of the bedroom floor. She bid a terse goodnight and went into her bedroom.

Emma pulled the satin bedclothes over her chest and thought about the day. The events spun through her head, almost causing severe vertigo. Despite two heavy dose sleeping pills, she was able to clearly relive Tom's visit during the funeral service and Travis's kiss.

And a cosmic bodyguard sent to protect her from a spirit world that held some sort of murderous grudge. The very same spirit entities that probably had murdered Tom and Karl Michael. Now she was next. Was that the inference she got from Shell?

Before she slipped into a deep sleep, she saw the bust of Valentino sitting on the mantle of the bedroom fireplace. Her last thoughts were of Valentino, knowing that somehow he was involved in Tom's death, and for some strange reason, she bore him no ill will.

She woke several times from sleep with tears splashing down her face onto a damp pillow. Tom was gone. She cried through the night.

Emma dressed in a pair of tan cotton shorts and a Kelly green polo shirt. Her reflection from the mirrors in the changing closet held a vacant face, drawn and strained. She looked frail and bone-thin.

Skillfully applying blush on her hollow cheeks, she was momentarily absorbed by the transparency of her fragile skin. The contrast of red lipstick against the pallor of her face startled her.

Walking by the spare bedroom, she noticed the door was open. She walked in. Shell was naked with his back turned to her. He was far more heroic in muscular size when stripped of clothes. He was bent over pulling clothes from one of the athletic bags. She stood quietly deciding how to slip away from his room gracefully.

"It's okay. I don't have anything to hide." He turned facing her, a boyish grin spread across his handsome face.

She blushed a deep crimson red. The moment was made more uncomfortable for her when she tried to look him in the face, lamely avoiding staring at his nakedness.

"My body selection was out of sentiment. Had it for thirty years till I was killed in the Great War, World War I to you, and I couldn't resist picking it to come back with. I was a dirt poor, hard working

English farm lad with four small sons. I understand I have quite a few great-grand kids now, but I'm not allowed to make contact with them. Gemma, my wife then, recently said I probably would have sired more children, but life and the king's war, and the other stupid things that men do to each other, along with the hard life of a farmer, probably would've taken me before I was thirty-five anyway."

Emma was more confused than ever. "You really meant what you said last night?"

"It's the truth." Robert continued looking into his athletic bag. He found a pair of black under shorts and pulled them through his legs.

"Well, you also said that you didn't eat. I was going downstairs to fix coffee and toast."

"Oh, I'll eat with you. I never have a human hunger for food or drink, but I like to appear mortal and honestly, I rather enjoy the ceremony of eating. One good thing though, I never gain or lose any weight." He chuckled.

He joined her at the kitchen breakfast table. She raptly watched him devour mounds of scrambled eggs and ham, toast, juice and several mugs of coffee while wondering where the food went.

"You are an incredibly beautiful woman, Emma. Your thoughts are even more beautiful than your physical body. You didn't let your early life turn you into a permanently bitter woman, and you survived despite setbacks, besting your environment."

Shell moved back from the table, "I'd love to make love to you--wish I could, but I can't, besides, it's not allowed anyway, a real waste of the equipment I'm packing, but I do think you need me for protection and a shoulder to lean on. The conflagration will be coming soon."

That was all she needed to let loose her build up of emotions, Emma sobbing from the pain and despair over Tom's undeserved and ugly death. Robert buried her in a hard protective embrace while he gently stroked her hair, Emma noticing his body smelled like a mountain meadow in a warm sun.

He scooped her into his arms, carrying her upstairs to the master bedroom, where he tenderly placed her under the bedcovers. They lay in a tight embrace while Emma softly poured out the pain and grief that shook her body. He held her until she drifted into sleep, then cautiously slid out of bed.

The angel went into the garden where he sat down facing the sun, reviewing his mission--and the sex he wished he could have had. Temptation was a hard thing to deal with, he thought, then sighed as the warmth from the sun washed over his five hundred earth year old body. Shell stood up from the chair and pulled off his shirt.

Mrs. MacClean watched the heavily muscled young man from her bedroom window overlooking Emma's backyard. She shook her head in indignation over Emma's forging a liaison so quickly after Tom's death, chalking it up to a total lack of breeding.

Chapter 15

The days winged by without discussion of Tom's death, a precious resting period enabling Emma time to cauterize her wounds.

She knew what she had to do during this healing period--the scattering of Tom's ashes. Emma had had Tom's remains cremated as soon as the service was over and after his empty casket was buried in the family plot at Fairmont Cemetery—cremation had always been his wish.

Emma drove alone to the summit of Mount Evans on a beautiful, cloudless day. A day filled with the bright sunshine of life and warmth, and despite the altitude of the mountain, the hour she took spreading his ashes across the mountain peak was surprisingly windless this day.

A stunningly beautiful day for an action of love. Tears continued to run down her cheeks while she dispersed small handfuls of his ashes; several times she paused and remembered their time together and the little things that had bonded their special love and passion.

They had lived together like an older and very passionate married couple, comfortable with each other and nothing left to prove, yet somehow settled in their ways, wary of any discussion that could open the door on secrets best left closeted.

Discovering Shell's supernatural abilities, Tom's transformation and the thoughts of what he would be doing in the afterlife, her first love, Travis, and the difficult journey of finding herself, Emma knew that even a script writer for a television soap opera would be frustrated in an attempt to plot this story.

Detective Shell worked grinding hours investigating and solving long-forgotten murder cases, any which could have the downside of exposing him to increased, and obviously unwanted media celebrity.

Emma threw herself onto charitable committees and university functions while wrapping up the final research on her Doctoral thesis. She had also formally notified the university of her intent to instruct in the upcoming winter quarter.

The confusion continued. Robert was a messenger and spirit guide from the Otherside, perhaps even an angel. On the surface he appeared to be too human. He snored, showered and shaved, "To keep in practice." He belched, fussed with his clothes and liked to tell slightly off-color jokes, jogged miles every day and lifted free-weights on a daily basis.

All of these human functions and traits totally bewildered her because he seemed to be very mortal, at times too mortal, and she had to constantly remind herself that he was not. Robert did not use a toilet or indicate, outwardly, the faintest interest in sex; he lacked any type of body odor, yet strangely smelled like a pristine morning. Not even a haircut was needed for his thick wavy, black hair.

His enormous appetite was also artificial, but he still enjoyed the taste and texture of food, and the sensation of having a full stomach. Shell also liked drinking large quantities of beer, "I get a fantastic human like buzz with no hangover."

Whenever Emma looked at his romance novel-cover face, framed by wavy raven-black hair, his solid athletic body poured into tight jeans and a polo shirt, she had to fight off less than spiritual thoughts.

Robert's articulate use of words and grammar, flavored with a faint Chicago accent and laced with American idioms, was another curious thing. If he had been a common English farmer, raised in an isolated corner of turn-of-the-last century England,

and probably uneducated considering the times, she wondered what had happened to his rural English accent and absence of dated colloquial phrases and words. His courtly manner and obviously educated mind deepened the mystery.

She felt comfortable living with this spirit guide, angel, or whatever he was. And safe. Also, Shell enjoyed laboring in the houses' extensive flower beds and lawn, appearing at his best doing mortal things like lawn mowing and house repairs, sweating profusely like a man doing heavy labor, yet he had been deceased since 1917.

At times, she almost felt married again. Telephone calls from Tom's acquaintances, still hoping to hit on a vulnerable, well-heeled widow, abruptly ended with Robert's deep voice answering the phone. The house appeared to be free of malevolent spirit intruders; she also had an agreeable companion to talk with and serve as an escort to social functions. He always had a sunny disposition and was never moody. She had the best of all possible worlds, and she totally ignored the snatches of gossip she heard about their living together.

"The two of us are going to take a few days off."

Emma looked up from the plate of delicious

roast beef and Yorkshire pudding that Shell had miraculously prepared in less than twenty minutes.

"I'm sorry, what did you say?"

"I said, we're taking a few days off--It's time."

Emma noticed his boyish face was holding a grin, his eyes twinkling.

"It's time for what?"

Robert finished nursing a stout mug of tea before replying. "We're going on a quick trip...beyond anything in your belief system. I think you're ready."

Her heart skipped a beat. Somehow she knew where they might be going. "A quick trip to where?" Knowing what was coming, she stalled him for composure. Emma rose from the table on the pretense of refilling the teapot.

"Sit down, Emma. Look at me. We're going to where I came from. We think the time is right, especially if you're going to find real purpose in your life."

The words 'we' and 'purpose' made her swallow hard. She coughed into her napkin. "Is it a must that I know?"

"Dear Emma, it's not going to hurt, matter of fact, I think you will rather enjoy your visit to those so-called Elysian Fields."

"Elysian Fields? You're kidding, the ancient

Greek version of eternal paradise? Well, do I really have a choice?"

"No, actually you don't."

They spent the rest of the evening discussing and butting heads over what she could expect, conversation becoming so unnerving that Emma jumped to her feet, nervously pacing back and forth while sorting through her thoughts. Desperately afraid of losing her grip on reality, she felt threatened with too many possibilities, what she had understood as dogma throughout her life were not empirical facts. Her recent exposure to paranormal events had taught her that life and death concepts went much deeper, the refinements in the supernatural world—the parallel universe, according to the unearthly Robert Shell, blew everything away—-totally.

Emma thrilled at a trip that few were allowed to embark on as an observer, and she was alive on top of it! At least she could come back! Millions or billions of human beings had permanently visited the Elysian Fields, Summerland, heaven, or whatever they called it, crossing directly over the astral plane bridge when it was their time. Even the thought of a specially guided tour through the unknown was still a terrifying thought.

He laughed, reading her thoughts. "I promise

we'll come back in one piece, you still have much to do before your time is over."

They would depart the following evening.

That evening came fast. In the living room, Robert took her delicate hands in his powerful plowman's hands. "Ready?" It was more of a command than a request.

Emma nervously cleared her throat, speaking in a reed-thin voice, "Ready as I'll ever be, yes, I'm ready."

"Then we shall call in the energy of the White Light. I want you to think it, see it, and feel it."

They chanted the invocation in unison: "We bring the Cosmic Forces into our bodies, asking for the White Light's strength, protection and guidance." At the conclusion of the sixth repeat of the invocation, they zoomed into a totally dark void. No dimension, no lights, no time or space, vectoring at speeds faster than any known earthly physics calculation.

They stood in the middle of a grassy meadow. No wind or breeze was occurring, nor the sight of a sun or moon, yet it was sunshine bright. Deep forests of variegated shades of green splashed with silver mist surrounded the endless meadow. The sky was fused in shades of opalescent blue. The shimmering grass was ankle high, sweet smelling and immaculate. A delicate fragrance hung in the still air, mixing with the sweet smells of a meadow. Although the sky was bright, Emma noticed that their bodies cast no shadows.

She focused her eyes on the surrounding countryside. Undulating tints of yellow-green, misty-brushed meadows and softly rolling hills were covered with profusion's of unknown flowers and strange trees, none being deciduous or conifers.

At first glance the landscape seemed void of animal life, later she saw herds of grazing dog-sized white deer, and flocks of strange looking rainbow-hued birds darting from tree to tree. She also noticed that the trees were hundreds of feet tall, much taller even than the mighty sequoias she had seen along the coasts of Oregon and Northern California.

She was immediately overcome by feelings of a peace that bordered on bliss, a state of being she had not experienced in a very long time.

"Magnificent isn't it?" She looked at Robert to

acknowledge his statement. He radiated a violet, flame-red aura; actually she could not decide what color it was.

"Look at your aura." Emma saw the yellow-orange rays that completely covered her body, vibrating with a pulsating energy which seemed to discharge from every cell and pore in her physical body. The fusion of energy and matter suspended her body several inches above the meadow grass.

"See the lake through that grove of trees?" She followed his pointing finger. "I want you to think that we're there--now."

They were there. The lake was serene, the stationary clouds above the still lake water were reflected as fleecy, cotton blobs. She looked again at the sky not remembering seeing clouds. The sky was cloudless.

"Things can be completely deceiving here." Robert was smiling at her.

Emma was growing increasingly light-headed with the beauty of the placid surroundings. She asked him, "Why are we here?"

"This is the second level of the astral planes. The first plane level is fairly close to earth and where earth-bound spirits are suspended. This plane is one of several where a departed soul comes if they aren't marked by evil, suicide, murder, greed, et cetera.

Emma, you are here to bear witness that this paradise does indeed exist. This is also the place where your psychic energies come from."

Emma listened, wanting to spring a question that darted through her mind. She was given the opportunity when Shell paused, "Where are the millions of souls who passed over to this plane?"

"They're here." He smiled knowingly while they hung suspended above the lake.

"It will become clear. First, I want you to use this cup to drink from the lake." He produced a small, translucent glass cup with a flourish of his hands, thrusting it at her. "Drink," adding, "Please." He pointed to the lake.

With out any hesitation, Emma bent down and scooped the rainbow-hued lake water into the cup. She paused before drinking the water, distracted by multi-colored flashing lights dancing in the cup. She drained the contents in two quick gulps. The water held a light fragrance of roses but tasted like cold spring water. Instantly she felt a surge of energy flash through her body.

"Wow!" Emma was overpowered with the sensation of an electrical-like current charging her entire body.

"You have now drunk of the waters on your own

free will, and surely the benefits will flow and let you see." His phrasing was a stilted invocation.

She joked, "Does this mean I'll also become much younger now? You know, banishing wrinkles, sags, those kinds of things?"

He laughed. "Sorry, my dear, there is nothing in the universe that can halt the natural order. You will be healthier than you have ever been, and far more astute and alert, if that is possible. Perhaps you will even notice a regeneration of brain cells and tissues, a pick-up of strength, but I'm sorry, your physical body will continue to age."

Shell was glowing with a brilliant intensity. Sparks of blinding light shot from the top of his head. "This is the lake whose water continues to jump-start the human race, as it has for many thousands of years. This is the water that can rebirth singular souls, as well as the souls of nations. These are the waters that create miracles for those in need. It is not necessary to drink from the lake itself, but only to believe that there exists a true source of goodness."

Emma left the side of Robert and wandered through the forests and the vast meadows, overcome with the astounding ethereal beauty she would have to eventually leave. She remained in a state of awe.

"You'll come back someday, when and if you

remain true to your mission." Shell's eyes focused on a thick grove of trees to their left, then smiled. "She's here, your control. I guess I should clarify what I mean, your temporal spirit guide, not to be confused with me, your personal, humble guardian angel." He almost laughed.

Emma squinted while her eyes searched the grove of glittering trees. A burst of light had suddenly materialized in the darkness of the verdant trees, which quickly drew towards them. In a quick blink of Emma's eyes a young woman in her early twenties seemed to appear within a few feet of where they floated.

Her diminutive figure was draped in a gold threaded spirit robe. Her waist length, lustrous black hair was complimented by large luminescent black eyes set in a fragile, high cheek-boned face.

Without waiting for Shell to introduce her, she blurted out, "Emma, my name was Carmella Franzia. I will be your liaison with this side for the rest of your earth-plane life. I will tell you a few facts about myself so that you will feel comfortable with me."

Emma felt dizzy and overpowered with the realization that this moment was not a dream.

Carmella continued. "I was a foolish young thing in my previous life, a silly, silly girl who stupidly challenged the Bishop of Padua, Italia, in 1803 with my visions and his indiscretions. He murdered me with his own hands when I refused to remain silent. You are my first earth-plane medium, but I promise you faithfully that we will be good partners."

"I don't think I understand. What do you mean, I will be a medium?"

Carmella held Emma's hands. "Dear Emma, through your maternal line, and for many generations now, you have carried the gifts of mediumship and the ability of trance. Your birth right can no longer be denied. You must help people transition and assist them in understanding the passing of their loved ones. You will lend credibility to the hundreds of people you make contact with, showing them that life does continue--if in several different forms." She looked deeply into Emma's inner Third Eye, then shifted her gaze to Robert.

Emma blushed at the lustful thoughts she had for Shell--her 'angel', especially sure that Carmella had discovered these feelings while probing her with those eyes...all knowing eyes.

Carmella had read her thoughts. "Don't be ashamed, it's only natural that the sexes are attracted to each other. Indeed, Robert Shell was a most beautiful man when he was mortal. She smiled, while continuing to hold Emma's hands. Carmella's hands were warm and strangely solid.

Another question surfaced in Emma's thoughts: 'Why hadn't Robert talked about his previous wife and children, who surely were dead by now, and were now supposedly in this paradise.' With that thought she looked at Shell, who knew what she was thinking, but he remained silent. Things would be revealed when they were meant to, he reasoned.

Carmella continued, "You have a great talent, with the potential of being one of the most talented mediums in your world. People will not scorn such a famous scholar as you, just because you work with the spirit world. I am most excited about the progress that you will make...as soon as you clear up the matter of the bracelet of that rascal, Rudolph Valentino!"

"What can I do? Can you help me with Valentino?"

"No! Since you live on the earth-plane with those demons, you must solve these problems with your growing talents. It's the only way these things are allowed to end." She could read the doubt in Emma's eyes. "You will work it out my dear one-- have faith."

Carmella turned to Robert. "Did I talk too much?"

Shell smiled, his perfect white teeth absorbing the reflection of Carmella's robe. "No, but thank you Carmella, you have been very helpful."

"Very good! I will leave you." She looked at Emma. "No further questions, at least for now. I am most happy to meet you. We will never meet again at this Summerland, but I will guide you during all earthly séance sittings and in your dreams. Robert will remain with you until you are completely safe."

Carmella imploded into a pin-point of searing light, flying like a drunken firefly into the forest.

"God, this is overwhelming! Is this real?"

"Yes, Emma, very real, more real than anything on your

plane. Shall we leave?"

"Actually, Robert, I'd rather stay." She meant it.

"Sorry, not your time…yet."

The month sauntered by. Emma remained expectant and found herself in continuous good humor. She felt as if she was under close scrutiny, and when Donna visited, Emma told her in hushed tones not to swear, talk about sex with Jack Sewell, or even smoke. She was uptight until Robert talked to her.

"Please don't change your habits or daily routine just because you know what I am and where you've been. We don't judge. Perfection is simply too hard to achieve for mortals, over here as well as over there."

She became relaxed and at ease after a few days, still averting her eyes whenever she passed his bedroom. He had, on several occasions innocently wandered naked through the house. Red-faced over seeing a physically perfect naked male--an angel, no less, Emma would chase after him with a bath sheet, afraid he would again answer the door in the buff, or pick-up the newspaper in the driveway.

They had late afternoon philosophical and metaphysical discussions over tea as often as she could corral him. Unknown to Emma, Shell immensely enjoyed these tea times, the special English teas with mounds of finger sandwiches, Scones and fruit tarts, that Emma had prepared especially for him. It was a comfortable period of introspection and relaxation for both, in which they discovered a lot about each other.

"What is life about? I mean, why do we struggle, get hurt, die, then start over again?"

"Dearest, adversities do strengthen fiber and resolve...gives proof of how well the pudding was cooked. If your mettle is weak, bitter and angry, then you could possibly become an earth-bound entity. Your life--and every creature's life in this great cosmos is a stepping stone to the astral planes, the real proving grounds. Some fail, some make it. It just is."

"Well then, how do we overcome the Akashic records or life events if everything is supposedly pre-written? It's going to take me a while to assimilate the un-understandable aspects of these Akashic records, because it's damn difficult to visualize some sort of a library floating around in this infinite universe where our personal destinies are recorded."

"Do you remember when you were in school, and were taking mathematics, with the problems in the front of the book, and the answers in the back of the same book? You had to work out the problems the long way to reach the known answer. Life is the same thing. The final answer remains the same despite the different ways taken to solve the problem. It's the same with the Akashic records."

Shell leaned back in the wing-backed chair and gobbled down another cucumber sandwich in his powerful hands while Emma filled their cups with hot Earl Grey tea.

"Another question: Why can I see you--you know what I mean, and uh, why are you so solid? An angel--really? And where are your wings anyway?"

"I'm a solid for the present, meaning I appear as real flesh and bones. My vibrational force is strong enough to give the appearance of this solidness. Mainly I'm discarnate, no physical body. I don't really think you'd be very comfortable if I was just a voice and a ghostly flicker. The wings you'll understand later."

Emma was reeling from this particular three hour long conversation. "This is more than I can handle, my brain is overloaded. Do you mind if I go to bed?"

"Don't mind at all. However, you must know that eventually we will have to talk about the next step, and I hope the final séance concerning our little Valentino problem."

"Do we have to? Really?"

"Emma, these malevolent spirits are only out of your hair at the moment, only because I'm here. We must get to the root of this nintety year old problem--way too many deaths. I now know that through your growing powers, and with Carmella's abilities, that we can clean up this matter once and for all. If you have any lingering reticence about this, I want you to remember what happened to Karl Michael, and of course, Tom. Jack Sewell might be next."

In the morning she was rested, not enough to leave bed, but enough to scan several research books on primitive cultures heaped high in bed. She drowsed into half sleep thinking of Tom, abruptly awaking with Robert at the side of the bed, holding a breakfast tray.

"I thought it was time to wait on you for a change. I hope the coffee is okay. The toast is a little scorched, but heck, it's my first time with a toaster. The scrambled eggs were easy. Sleep okay?"

He sat on the side of the bed, and they shared the coffee, toast, orange juice, and Strawberries in cream. He beamed when she wolfed the food down.

The better part of her day was spent in the university Penrose library, collecting final material for the paper that she had been assured by the department chairman, would be published. Emma grimaced at the thought of the many long, grueling hours she had already spent researching the insipid academic material that Dean Wade, chair of the

VALENTINO'S CURSE

Anthropology Department and her sponsor, had assigned over three years ago. It was a hellish ritual to become a full professor, and in lieu of everything that happened—was futile.

That was several years ago, ancient history now. There once had been a time when she would have gladly cart-wheeled naked across campus to get her professorship. And now? Rather doubtful and moot. Emma snorted at the innocuous assigned title: 'The Invisible World Of Sorcerers And Shamans Of Three Cultures: Mayan, Arunta And Benin'.

She groaned. Most of the books she needed had been checked out by the School of Theology. She did not intend to walk half way across the campus in blast furnace-heat to fetch and beg the books she needed.

Emma found an empty study carrel with a functioning desk lamp in the back stacks, and plopped down with five heavy books.

Pulling out three new spiral notebooks and a handful of sharpened red pencils from a book bag, and being a compulsive Virgo, she neatly straight lined the pencils next to each other over the scarred desk.

Three hours limped by with an attempt to focus on the material. Occasionally She would look up at distractions that snaked through her weak concentration; she would give a cursory disapproving look to the offender, then resume jotting notes in a scrawl she would later find incomprehensible.

Deciding to end three hours of non-productive twitching, she packed the pencils and notebooks into the canvas book bag and made her way to the check-out counter. Three of the books were outdated and barely fit the subjects she was researching, but she felt the book's bibliographies might give her leads on other material. She made a resolve to visit the Tattered Cover Bookstore on Saturday and order sixteen of the books she needed, figuring it was time to update her home library. Emma was positive that the Internet would be of little use.

A wasted day, even at her favorite natural food store. The Hawaiian Kona coffee was on backorder, the imported Dutch Edam cheese was out of stock, and the meat cutter proclaimed that he had been waiting all day for the delivery of the organically fed free-range chickens. Emma propelled herself to the front door of the house, fumbled with the door key pad and cursed under her breath. She was hot and further exasperated because the car had stalled out two times on University Boulevard on her way home, and during rush hour. Tom had warned her that the BMW was long overdue for servicing, something he had always taken care of; she sighed at his memory.

She remembered her college roommate's poster: 'A woman needs a man like a fish needs a bicycle'. She laughed then, now she felt otherwise. A man around the house helped to cushion the sting of living alone, and being at the mercy of automobile mechanics, lawn work, home repairs, and setting out the garbage.

Obviously, she thought, radical feminists felt nothing for the day-to-day support women needed to survive the difficulties of a hostile environment. A loving male in bed was also nothing to sneer at. A feminist could have it both ways she decided long ago, a little compromise here and there never weakened basic beliefs or character.

After searching the first floor for Robert she remembered his rusting gray Jeep Laredo was not in the driveway. He probably was on duty investigating the recent front-page murder of a Capitol Hill real estate developer. She laughed to herself, hating the thought of running up against a spirit investigator.

Shell miraculously solved every assigned case, no

matter how stale the case was or obscure the trail. She mused at his obvious supernatural powers, and how strange it was that not one person in the media or police department had questioned his perfect record in solving the unsolvable, completely on his own, in days or hours, where teams of detectives and smug FBI agents had failed.

The answering machine held eleven messages from people requesting her support on benefit and fund-raising committees, solicitations for donations, and three frantic messages from Donna.

Donna had given her a pager the previous Christmas. Emma refused to carry the pager in her purse, knowing the device would be constantly beeping with Donna's calls. She knew if she called, Donna would be hot over her non-response to the pager, which was presently buried under junk in a kitchen drawer. Emma carried the pager only when she was with Donna and the cell phone from Tom was somewhere in the trunk of her car.

After draining the cup of herbal tea, she pulled off her sneakers and laid down on the family room couch, eyes too heavy and mind too drowsy to scan the small mountain of mail. She was in a deep sleep in less than three minutes.

"Hey, you. Time to get up."

VALENTINO'S CURSE

She opened her eyes at Robert's baritone voice. He sat in the chair across from the couch.

"I made a reservation for dinner tonight. Are you too tired to go out?"

She was now fully awake. "No, I would like to get out of the house tonight. Where are we going? Do I need to dress up?"

"Whoa. Nothing formal, if that's what you mean. You know how much I like to dress up."

She flashed through the bedroom while quickly applying a light touch of blush to her high cheekbones, and a dab of lipstick on her thin lips; she primped her hair in less than a minute, pulled and kicked off her sweatshirt and jeans on the dressing closet floor. She hurriedly shimmied into a navy blue skirt and a white silk blouse, checked her makeup and primped her hair again. A flush of pink Coral earrings and a matching strand of Coral beads completed her toilet.

"You are beautiful." He meant it.

"Thank you." And she meant it.

Emma's heart fluttered over how handsome he was. Despite being dressed in a European body-tailored dark brown blazer and a loose fitting chocolate-colored silk shirt, she dared a cliche, Robert looked clean-cut and all-American. Robert Shell, an exalted guardian angel, her personally assigned angel, could have brought out the most venial lust from even the most bitter of spinsters.

Jake's Place topped the twelve story hotel that hugged the side lip of a steep hill overlooking the Denver Basin. Smog absorbed the waning rays of dusk, splashing a flamingo pink and brilliant milk-orange tint over the fading, purple mountains crouching in the shadows to the west of the city. The vast twinkling ribbons of the metro-area city lights magnified an already surrealistic landscape.

He ordered a four course dinner for two; lemon scallops for an appetizer, salmon bisque soup, a mixed green salad with watercress dressing, and fillets of sole stuffed with marinated pop-corn shrimp. A bottle of estate-bottled wine complimented each course.

They savored the meal in silence.

Before desert, Emma asked, "Robert, where ever did you acquire your jaded tastes?" She was not taunting, but she could see that he was slightly annoyed at the comment.

No response. He only smiled.

"Please forgive me. I didn't intend to sound bitchy."

"I know, and forgiven. In response to your

question, you know I've been around for more than a few years. I picked up some rather degenerate tastes when I was on assignment in France. What would you like for desert?"

"Oh, no. I'll pop. You go ahead." She actually wanted a raspberry cream brule, but thought she wanted to preserve her size six.

Shell ordered a plate of five chocolate raviolis swimming in a thick raspberry sauce and a side snifter of brandy.

Emma gazed deeply into his lustrous eyes, made even more bewitching by the flickering candlelight. "Now tell me. I know this night was meant to be more than a night out with an excellent dinner."

"Good guess. Coffee?" She declined with a quick nod. He pulled his chair closer to the table. "I've got a wonderful surprise for you. It took considerable restraint on my part to hold back until I was given the okay."

A sweating violinist stopped at their table, and seemed to leer with several missing teeth while he played, 'I'll Be Seeing You'. Robert reached into his breast pocket and pulled out a black leather billfold. The violinist flashed a pumpkin-like grin and bowed at the $20 bill, quickly strolling to the next table before Robert changed his mind.

"You're driving me crazy. What surprise?"

"You're now able to get pregnant."

She winced, then softly gasped. Emma knew Robert would never lie, but she also knew she was incapable of having children, several miscarriages had proven this. Even if impregnation were possible, which it wasn't, insemination went beyond the rational in her current physical state. How could she ever possibly get pregnant with the damage that had been done when she was a young girl?

"Are you playing games? Several specialists and many tests said I had far too much scar tissue from my, eh..."

"I know what happened to you in that foster home, trust me when I say that it was psychological and not physical."

She was elated in spite of strong disbelief. "It's not possible...no. Ha, Tom was the last man I was involved with. If I couldn't get pregnant from him—no, I can't believe it. I'm too old anyway. Impossible! No!" She almost shouted.

"Emma, how many times have I told you that nothing is impossible in this universe, especially with 'special' assistance.

She was on the verge of tears. "Please, don't say anymore.""It's our gift. A reward. Emma, believe me, it's true. If all goes the way we've planned, in less than a year you'll be a full professor and will meet a scholastic type at the university—a sterling fellow you already know, and, I might add, you will love him. You will have children."

She laughed out loud in pain and denial. "Oh hell, I don't know what to say!" Emma knew that Robert could not tell lies.

They were quiet while they drove home. She looked out the window at the passing scenery without seeing. When they arrived home she went directly to her bedroom without talking to Robert and crawled into bed without undressing. She cried herself to sleep, wishing that children had come from Travis or Tom, a fervent wish she had kept buried in secret.

Emma awakened the following morning to Robert's clattering in the kitchen. She rose from bed, stretched, then walked into the bathroom. Wrung out from the shock of last night, she drew water for a bath.

The steam from the hot water filled the bathroom, then remembering what she had read in a magazine about the dangers of a hot bath to women especially ones who were trying to get pregnant, she turned off the hot water and waited until the bath water was tepid. She daydreamed about children, while making plans.

After a leisure bath she pulled on a pair of jeans and a tattered gray University of Denver sweatshirt while she made her way to the kitchen. She felt limp from the bath and what Shell had said the previous night—actually, Emma felt elated.

"Well, good morning to you. Did you sleep well?" He smiled, reading her thoughts.

She answered, almost singing, "I'm still in a state of disbelief, can't imagine why, can you?"

He was sitting at the kitchen table sipping coffee.

She forced herself to remain calm. "Something smells good."

"Ground some fresh coffee. I cooked you some sausages and your favorite blueberry pancakes. Have a seat." He went to the stove where he had kept her breakfast warm.

Emma ate in silence while he thumbed through the morning newspaper. "This is very good. Where did an angel learn to cook?"

"It's something that even we learn to do, especially if they once lived on earth."

He remained quiet until she was through eating. "Emma, Jack Sewell will be calling in a few minutes. He'll want you to be the medium at a séance next Wednesday night, and I want you to say yes. It's the only way to send them back, once and for all. Think of Jack's life, possibly even yours."

She had few reservations. It had to be done. Tom's death had to be repaid, regardless of any Karma she might pick up. She did not intend to forget or banish the anger she felt toward the entities. There had to be a pay-back.

He read her thoughts, "Vengeance is never a solution." She agreed to be the medium when Jack called.

Chapter 16

The sitting group assembled Wednesday night at the church. Emma, Jack, Donna, Robert, Lucia Swenson, and her husband, Erick.

They sat in the waiting room next to the séance room, while Robert went over the ground rules. Although Jack Sewell was the leader of the church and the supposed most experienced medium at the gathering, Jack sensed Shell's considerable powers.

Shell stood in the center of the group, dressed in a loose fitting black silk shirt and black pleated linen trousers. He carefully chose his words while he scrutinized every face slowly, then smiled when he had screened their thoughts.

"This sitting is very important, quite possibly the most important séance that you have ever participated in. Two lives have been taken because we didn't take the malevolence of these entities seriously enough. Two additional lives are possibly in jeopardy, Jack's and Emma's. I admire your courage for being here." Shell was silent for a few minutes while he waited for his words to lend an impact to his statement.

He continued. "What you'll see tonight is close to being an exorcism. It will be unnerving, frightening...and could be quite dangerous. The very incarnation of evil will gather in the next room, trying to separate us from our resolve. I want all of you to be sure, very sure, that you want to participate. If any of you don't feel that you want to risk this danger, you may go now without any condemnation." He paused while he searched each mind for signs of doubt.

He waited several minutes before he spoke again. "Good, the vibrations I feel from each of you is impressive. Let me continue. Somehow, these earth-bound entities have grown more powerful and willful. It appears they have grown into a powerful mass, and into a very dangerous one."

Shell paused while he composed his words under the guise of drinking from a glass of water. "I know Jack reviewed the events of the past weeks, but I will again emphasize the heart of the problem. Emma's grandmother was given a gold bracelet during a séance in 1926, it seems by Valentino's spirit. We have no idea why he gave this gift to her, but it has been a curse to Emma's maternal line ever since. We suspect the lives of Karl Michael and Tom Glass were snuffed out because they found the answer. It does not appear the spirit of Valentino is causing this grief, but one spirit in particular is. All of the answers are known to us, the clues, I suspect, are under our noses. Tonight we must drive these entities away...by the sheer force of our abilities. We will have a short break then Jack will explain the rules of our sitting."

Emma and Donna left the room while Donna had a cigarette.

"I wasn't going to come tonight, Em, but I knew it was important for you and Jack. The sight I've garnered over three years has always frightened me, don't get me wrong, I've used it for others, and of course for myself. I'm just damn afraid of the evil we will face tonight."

Donna took a deep drag on her cigarette then watched the smoke drift above her head. Emma also watched the puff of smoke dissipate.

"Why did you really come?"

Donna looked into her eyes. "Dad came to me in my dream last night, looked wonderful. He said I must attend. That was all I needed. In life he never asked much of me, but I could tell he wanted me here. I like Jack very much, and love you, so I guess I'm here of my own free will, with encouragement, of sorts."

Emma felt the sincerity of her statement. They hugged each other.

"I'm still scared shitless, honey."

Emma laughed. "Me too, since I'm going to be the medium."

"No! Good grief, no wonder you've been so quiet!"

They filed into the séance room and sat down at the table. Emma sat between Robert and Donna, Donna sitting next to Erick Swenson, his wife, Lucia, then Jack Sewell and Robert. A complete circle of six people with supernatural abilities, one with immortal spirit power far and above the other five mortal beings. Jack spoke. "The rules of protection. Always think of the power of the White Light. No talking or touching the visitors. Never break the circle of hands. Emma will be our séance medium tonight. Trust her emphatically. Never, ever, leave the room during the sitting, and if you should feel faint, think of the power and the majesty of the White Light and the protection and guidance it gives. Ready?" He looked around the table, then satisfied, said, "Emma, we bind our hands and our hearts with yours."

Emma rose from the table and lit the large white candles sitting in wrought iron candelabras in each corner of the room. She picked up a crystal vase filled with long stemmed white Calla Lilies from a side table and placed them in the center of the oak table. Before she sat down, she dimmed the lights.

"Would everyone please take several deep breaths to clear your minds." She watched closely while deeply breathing. When satisfied, she said, "Join hands." Emma was completely relaxed and prepared; her heart was fluttering.

"I bring the energy of the White Light and its blessing, asking for its protection and guidance." She repeated the invocation until she could feel the vibrational force rise in the room. In minutes, the room was filled with pin-points of bright light which quickly fused into a silver cloud that hung suspended over the center of the table.

When she had completed the invocation, the silver-white cloud became a transparent sparkling mist that clung to the ceiling, walls and floor.

"Carmella, would you please ask Rudolph Valentino to join us." Emma's eyes were closed while she looked at Carmella in Summerland. Carmella was smiling, her lips moving, but Emma was unable to hear her voice. She repeated, "Carmella, would you please ask Rudolph Valentino to join us?"

Emma had supposed it was going to be difficult for Carmella to have Valentino quickly materialize, perhaps it would take a measure of cajoling by Carmella. Then she remembered. Rudolph Valentino was an earth-bound entity not in the dimension that comprised the second plane of Summerland! Would Carmella be able to do anything at all? Beads of perspiration formed on her forehead.

She slit her eyes and looked at the faces of the sitters around the table. Everyone was in a deep meditational state, all, except for Robert who was looking straight ahead, his copper eyes shining like a cat's caught in the headlights.

Valentino stood to the back of Lucia Swenson. He was looking directly at Emma while flashing a smile of perfect teeth.

"My dear, I understand you want me? His voice was more Italian-accented than she had remembered. The sound of his voice sliced through the morgue-quiet atmosphere of the room.

Emma shouted, "Please, don't break the circle!"

He appeared to be solid, dressed in an old-fashioned tailored black tuxedo, his black hair heavily pomaded and slicked to the back of his head. His short stature was athletic and wiry.

She admitted he was immensely handsome, looking far more masculine than he had in the silly studio photographs, or when she had first met him. Something was very different about him tonight though, he appeared more flesh and blood and no longer like a cardboard movie still.

Valentino struck a three-quarter profile while he pulled a gold cigarette case from the breast pocket of his tuxedo jacket. He freed a long, dove-gray colored Turkish cigarette, tapped it twice on the closed case, then thrust it into his thin lips. The cigarette end immediately lit on its own. Taking a deep pull on the cigarette he slowly exhaled through his nose while he continued to pose.

His voice was thick with sarcasm. "Now, what may I do for you? You called me, cara mia, remember?" His eyes momentarily flashed like ignited coals, then suddenly hooded in annoyed menace.

Emma spoke, "We want the end of your visitations and the spirits that seem to come with you."

"You really mean hauntings, don't you, sweet darling? Impossible, not until you solve the little riddle we gave you."

"We?"

VALENTINO'S CURSE

Valentino sighed for effect. He took another deep pull on the cigarette, then dropped it on the carpet where his heel ground it out. Contempt was evident in his body language. "Very well, we shall have to entertain you."

Tango music flooded the room from nowhere, slithering and cautious as it made its appearance in the heavy oxygen of the static-charged room; it became bold and quickly grew to an ear-splitting crescendo. The sitters tightly grasped each other's hands in fear, wanting to cover their ears but very much afraid of breaking the protective circle.

"Oh, it is rather loud," shouted Valentino. The music immediately dropped to comfortable human decibels. Tango dance music, loose and sensual. Valentino's Argentinean Gaucho music.

"Beautiful is it not?" Valentino strutted around the table to Jack's side.

"To all, may I present my beautiful former wife, Natacha Rambova."

She materialized at his side in the blinking of an eye. Natacha looked supple and sultry, shorter by an inch or two than Valentino. Her torso struggled to stay covered by a low scooped neck, white beaded evening dress that hit two inches above her knees. A boy's build, except for full breasts almost hidden under layers of dangling bugle-beaded strands. Her chestnut brown hair was bobbed. The only touch of makeup on her death-mask face was penciled eyebrows and a hot-red gash of lipstick. Natacha was the personification of a Roaring Twenties Vamp, and somehow a very dangerous one.

"Rudy, shall we perform a Tango for this dear audience?" Natacha's voice was full-throated and even in timbre.

Valentino scooped her up tightly into his arms, slowly loosening his hold with the passionate beat of the Latin music. They were one as they bent low, Valentino holding her inches above the floor. Slowly gliding in unison across the room, they drew closer, cheek-to-cheek, separating then joining with the hypnotic beat. Emma's heart fluttered in synchronization with the lush sensuality of their movements.

Robert leaned close to her ear, "Steady Emma, it's a dance of snakes."

With this warning, Emma abruptly shook the spell free. The music stopped as the spirit couple stood looking directly into her eyes.

"Touche, stupid bitch. We almost had you." Emma was annoyed and at the same time mortified with Natacha's venomous remark.

VALENTINO'S CURSE

"Perhaps it is now time to finish our little game."

Emma felt a blast of cold air enter the room. She shivered at the sudden drop of room temperature. She also observed the candle flames bravely flickering with the entry of the ice-cold draft.

Natacha floated closer to the table, searching Emma's eyes for the smallest hint of fear. "Darling, I see you are not afraid of me, why, I even see you have a sweet little peasant girl on the other side waiting to help you. Could it be Carmella?"

Her ice-blue eyes flashed with hatred. "Nothing will help you unless you solve this little puzzle. Your tedious, meaningless life will depend on it. Thanks to our silver screen idol, this mess will have to come to a conclusion this very night. Yes, something else. Look at my nails. Familiar?"

Emma almost went into shock when she looked at the finger nails thrust a few inches from her face. Long, well-manicured nails painted in lavender polish, capped on delicate hands. The fist at the séance, the hag clerk in the mountain store! Natacha Rambova!

The spirit of Natacha hissed. "You've got something I want! Dear Reba refused to give it back, and yes, your grand mother, and mother, all too stupid to realize that I meant business." She paused, looking at Valentino. "I don't know why I always have to bail you out of these fettles, my fine Italian darling."

Valentino grew angry. "Why do you always demean me? You almost ruined my career with...."

"Career, darling? You call those stupid movies you made a career? I tried to uplift your empty-headed trash to at least a passable art form..."

"And almost destroyed me! You took my money, used me, left me. Yes, you almost ruined me, but 'Son of the Sheik' showed my true talents, and without your so-called help!"

" 'Son of the Sheik' was trash!" Valentino was livid. Blood seemed to actually flush his handsome enraged face.

"You and your lesbian friends mocked me, using me...sucking me dry! Don't call my movies trash, just because you came from wealth. What did you ever accomplish in your life? You are only remembered because you were married to me, a lowly dago movie star!"

Natacha was silent. She stared at Valentino with blank eyes, the only emotion on her face being quivering nostrils.

Valentino continued. "I loved you dearly. I never

loved anyone as much as you. I did everything you told me. You took my soul when you divorced me, but that wasn't enough, was it? You poisoned me... even remarried a few years after my death. You were always so cold-hearted."

Natacha interjected. "Yes I did. If I couldn't have you...."

"You left me, love of my life, I didn't leave you!"

"It's no matter. You were vain, but likable in your male simpleness. Foolish and caught up with yourself. Neurotic and a show-off. You were always more aroused by a plate of pasta than a real woman. My dearest sheik, I hate to expose family secrets to everyone here, but you never even consummated our marriage, the world's greatest lover! Ha! You were always living a charade. Dago boy, the best part of you is below the belt and you didn't know how to use it. But, my Sheik of Arabia, I still love you in my own way, though. If you suspected that I was a lesbian, then why ever did you marry me?" She spat like a cat.

Valentino broke in. "Emma, I want you to know that Natacha poisoned me slowly with arsenic. Officially my death was listed as Peritonitis, from a burst appendix, but I was only 31 years of age, and in excellent health. My spirit guides, Meselope, Black Feather and White Cloud, warned me about what was going to happen--my early death, but I refused to believe that she would do this to me. I also want you to know that I had nothing to do with any of these deaths. She and her evil fiends did it. I have lingered on this plane because I want somebody to know why I...how I died. Natacha didn't think I knew about the arsenic she put in my food, and the Belgian chocolates she sent me for two years, all laced with arsenic--she even put it on my clothes. I hoped desperately that my love would eventually prevail over her evil."

"It doesn't really matter anymore, darling Rudy. You have been forgotten. Your coarse little fans are all dead now. You only exist in movie books and faded, quaint films that nobody sees."

Valentino was crestfallen.

Natacha spoke to Emma. "I want my slave bracelet back. It was for Rudy only, a sign of my special love...in my own fashion. I might even consider letting you and the others live, um, maybe, but only if you give it back. What is mine, remaines mine. Oh, this is too delicious!" She laughed shrilly.

Carmella was warning Emma about Emma's waning energy force, with less than a half hour left of strong vibrations to dip into. Emma was approaching the invisible plateau of exhaustion. Her intense vibrational strength was slowly dissipating, only energized because of Shell's and Carmella's extra reservoir of energy. Emma was worried, knowing closure had to occur. This would be the only chance to seal the cosmic door on Natacha and her fiends.

She decided to provoke Natacha. "I hate your filthy meddling in my life. You murdered my grandmother and then my parents, you sick bitch! Then Tom and Karl Michael! I only wish I had someway to properly repay you for the misery and suffering you've caused. All because of a cheap bracelet."

Natacha screamed, "You fool, I can make you suffer more than you'll ever know!"

"You couldn't possibly hurt me anymore than you already have!"

The room was suddenly filled with the gagging fragrance of a heavy floral perfume. Lucia Swenson and Jack coughed.

Emma recognized the fragrance. "That was you!"

"Of course, Lilies Of the Valley, and the finest I might add. It was my signature. You also ignored my other clue from the Ouija board, 'Winifred Shaughnessey'. My, for a person who delves in academic research, you certainly don't follow clues; several times I fanned the pages of Tom's book on movie history of this sad Italian immigrant's marriage to me, and even in my biography."

Shell's thoughts entered Emma's mind, warning her to commence the exorcism at once.

Emma snatched the heavy gold slave bracelet from her lap where it lay hidden in the folds of her skirt, throwing it to the middle of the table.

"Oh, you did bring it! You might not be as stupid as I thought. I gave it to him as a love offering, a symbol for all ages of our perfect love, then he throws it away as a grand gesture to the lowly Reba!"

Emma joined hands again with Robert and Donna while she commenced the invocation of exorcism, repeating word for word what Carmella was telling her.

"I ask the power of the White Light to dissolve the vibrations of Natacha Rambova and the malevolence of her kindred spirit forces from this earth plane. May their evil mass vanish with these words. May they rest forever in peace behind the Great Door, never to come back."

"What are you doing, stupid woman? There's nothing you can do to us!"

Everything happened in slow motion. Natacha

stood completely still with a look of disbelief and hatred smeared across her face. After Emma had repeated the invocation for the sixth time, she noticed Natacha's spirit growing transparent and out of focus.

The room grew cold as a meat locker. The sickly fragrance of Natacha's perfume clung to the cold air in the dank room. Two of the sputtering candle flames had snuffed out with the ice-cold draft that swirled throughout the room.

Emma lunged for the slave bracelet, throwing it into the icy mist now surrounding Natacha. It sounded like an electrical overload when it hit Natacha's apparition.

The White Light reassembled its flashing mass into a miniature electrical storm which waved above their heads, floating like an enormous Jellyfish in clear water. For a few minutes the living occupants in the room feared they had lost their gravity and were being sucked into some sort of a spirit black hole. The noise of sizzling electrical discharges grew deafening.

Natacha's mouth was open in a silent scream. As her apparition became milky-white and distorted, she screamed in obvious pain, low and guttural at first, then rising octaves to an ear piercing shriek, a shriek of pain, horrible enough to propel the sitters around the table into slapping hands over their ears. She vanished with Valentino; the Door was closed.

Emma's eyes swept the room. The only apparent signs of Natacha and Valentino's visit was the disappearance of the Calla Lilies that had been in the crystal vase in the center of the table, plus a crushed cigarette on the carpet. Carmella had told

Emma that Valentino's spirit was now free from Rambova's influence. He would be working on his own release as an earth-bound entity.

With the complete dissipation of her energy, Emma collapsed into Shell's waiting arms.

Chapter 17

Months after the séance, Emma wandered listlessly through the house and flower gardens. She was emotionally and physically exhausted, but strangely her mind felt refreshed and focused. She was cheerful, especially every time she thought about becoming pregnant. Donna and Jack faithfully stopped by every other day to check on her. They never made comments about Shell living in the house.

Robert was cheerful but also was becoming more and more detached. He would look over at her while they were eating, and when their eyes would meet, he would abruptly look down at his plate and resume picking at his food. She knew he had much to say but avoided any lengthy attempt at conversation.

Two weeks later, he finally approached her. "I'm leaving Emma. I would like to stay with you much longer, but I really have to go. My time on this plane is through; my mission is completed."

Tears welled in her eyes. "Do you really have to go?"

"Yes--this weekend. I resigned from the police department two days ago, I didn't want them bothering you with questions on my disappearance. I'm leaving the house and gardens in good shape. Emma, you're going to have a good life, and you will continue to grow so much spiritually--I have no doubt that we will meet again when it is your time."

Tears splashed down her face. "I'm going to miss you."

"If you only knew how much I want to stay, but it is not allowed."

He held her tightly in a smothering embrace while she cried. He smelled like rain-fresh fields in sunshine. "I know it's stupid of me to ask, but I'll ask it anyway. Can I see you as an angel, with your wings?"

He laughed, "Absolutely not, and anyway, wings are only for the romantically inclined who believe they must see wings, the only time they will ever see me in full uniform," he laughed at his comment, "Is when it's time to pass over, or when you're in distress."

VALENTINO'S CURSE

On Sunday, Robert left her a two page note on the kitchen table. Her hands shook while she read his masculine scrawl, 'Energy is indestructible. The departed come back when needed to help and inspire, offering the promise of an eternal life. The other side knows no injustice, social and class status, or illness, a place where we are all given a second chance. Think of it, an eternity where all souls are equal and wealth matters not!'

The note continued, 'I enjoin you to spread this message, If you were pretty sure of immortality, your immortality in particular, then wouldn't you live your life differently? Emma, show them the way. As your spirit guardian, your personal angel, I want you to know that I will always be near you. Tom knew me in that alley in Las Vegas, and now you have known me. I hope that I have made a difference, you have with me'.

On the last page of the note she didn't want to end, it said, 'I want to leave my favorite quotation with you, it might serve you well as a guide post: 'Appearances to the mind are of four kinds: Things either are what they appear to be, nor appear to be or they just are--and do not appear to be, or they are not'. Confused? Farewell, my dearest Emma'.

She absent mindly folded the sheets of paper

into eights, stuffing it into her rear jean pocket. Emma was depressed over his departure but lately had felt a growing exhilaration sweeping through her core: She had met her guardian angel! Her new beginning was a gift of intercession and forgiveness from the Cosmic Forces of the universe, a balance that would carry her through the rest of her natural earth life until it was time to embark on the real voyage. Now, instead of feeling alone, she would have others to share her mortal journey with.

She leaned against the gleaming granite counter, switching on the electric kettle of water, intensely craving the anticipated high of an oversized mug of caffeinated tea, speculating on the selected breeding male she would soon meet from the university.

Emma knew in advance the vitals about him: his name was James Concanso, was eight years younger than she, was an expert in spirit Electronic Voice Phenomenon, and was a new, fully vested professor in Italian Medieval History. It was questionable whether he was a mortal or not—she would find this out later, and he would give her three talented and healthy children, two boys and one girl.

She also was aware that they would make a stunning couple despite an apparent difference in age;

they would have three dates, and four sleep in's before they would be wedded.

Emma knew she had been granted another cat's life, and she grew more excited with the prospect of yet another exciting journey, especially since she was now very much aware of the rules handed down by the other side.

Emma sighed a comfortable release of gentle tension as she knew indeed, it was going to be a remarkable new journey. She made a vow that not only would she be an outstanding mother and wife, but would be the best séance medium ever envisioned.

She thought of all the tender souls that had been lost… All over a bracelet…

Breinigsville, PA USA
05 January 2011
252719BV00001B/16/P